WASTELAND MARSHALS

GAIL Z. MARTIN

LARRY N. MARTIN

Cover Design by Robyne Pomroy

This book is a work of fiction. Any resemblance to any person, living or dead, is coincidental. Except that bit about that guy. That's totally a thing.

1

"I miss pizza." Shane Collins looked up at the broken neon sign for the abandoned pizza restaurant with a sigh.

"The world practically ends, and you miss pizza?" Lucas Maddox echoed.

"Among other things," Shane replied. The mom-and-pop roadside motel they planned to squat in for the night sat across a crumbling highway from the old pizzeria, sparking memories and a pang of loss.

"Yeah, lots of other things," Lucas replied, as he finished checking out the empty motel lobby to assure no unwelcome surprises awaited them. Three years after a clusterfuck of epic proportions had effectively stopped the twenty-first century cold in its tracks, ruins like the old motel had become reminders of what had been.

"Hey, it's got a solid roof, the walls are cement block, and we can bring the horses into the utility shed overnight. We've done with worse," Shane pointed out.

Which was true, Shane thought. As partners in the US Marshals, they had spent many nights holed up in mid-price hotels safeguarding witnesses. Before that, in the Army, they'd survived miserable missions in bombed-out villages. The comfortable suburban childhood they'd shared as friends since elementary school was another relic of a world that no longer existed.

The two men were a study in contrasts, though they were both thirty-five and within a half inch of the same six-foot-two height. Shane was blond, with what Lucas always joked was an All-American cowboy look. Lucas had dark hair and eyes, rocking more of a bad boy vibe. That had made it easy when the job demanded playing good cop/bad cop.

"And the floor's tile. I never thought cheap motel carpet could get any worse—but it did," Lucas replied. A few years without heat or cooling turned most hotel guest rooms into breeding grounds for mold and wild animals. They had learned the hard way that the motel office usually made a better shelter—tile floor, less furniture, and good visibility. And in some cases, like tonight, a real fireplace.

Lucas had already poked and prodded at the flue until he felt sure that they could light a fire relatively safely. After a cold ride from their last waystation, he seemed positively giddy about the possibility.

"I brought in our bedrolls and saddlebags," Lucas said as he rose from where he knelt next to the 1970s-style hearth, dusting the soot off his hands. "There's some grass next to the parking lot that looks safe for the horses to eat. You want to take the horses over to graze, and then down to the pond, while I go looking for firewood?"

"Yeah, and I'll bring up a bucket of water to boil. Warm food would be a nice change."

He headed out to the gravel parking lot, where they had tied Lucas's black stallion and his own roan gelding. They had named them "Shadow" and "Red" respectively, unimaginative but functional, although they had long joked about more colorful names from the fantasy novels and games they liked, more along the lines of Sleipnir or Shadowfax. Shane had argued that both of those names took entirely too long to say, though the thought still made him smile.

"Come on you two. Let's get you fed and watered before it's full dark." Shane led their mounts over to the grass that stretched down to a small pond, then stood guard as they began to eat.

Three years ago, the idea of trading in their black SUV for a pair of horses would have prompted plenty of cowboy jokes and incredulous chuckles. Shane ran a hand along Red's side affectionately. He'd grown fond of both horses, although he'd probably always miss heat, air conditioning, and the protection from the elements he'd once taken for granted in the confines of a vehicle.

The pond was part of a small park. Its gazebo and playground looked to be in good shape, though the area was as deserted as the motel. Gazing at the green space gave Shane a peaceful feeling, something difficult to come by these days. He let himself enjoy the view, then frowned as he strained to make out music so distant that he couldn't be certain whether he had heard it or merely imagined the song. Shane looked all around but saw no one in sight. It seemed odd, but it wasn't the first time he'd had something like that happen. Shane chalked it up to his imagination and turned his focus back to the horses.

Lucas's shout broke Shane from his thoughts.

"Come on," he told the horses, tugging at their reins. He didn't dare leave them unprotected and loose, but Lucas needed his help. The horses came with him reluctantly, and he ran as fast as he could with them in tow, sending them into the relative protection of the shed he and Lucas had scouted earlier. He closed the door behind them and headed toward where the shouts had sounded.

He came around the corner, his crossbow drawn. Lucas was down, fighting for his life against a huge black dog. Only it wasn't a normal dog, Shane knew as he tried to get a clear shot where he could hit the attacker and not Lucas. A grim only looked like a large, ugly dog, the size of a sow with black, matted fur, bat-like ears, and red eyes. It was really a revenant, a supernatural creature, and so nothing but iron or silver would do the job.

Shane squeezed the trigger, sending a silver-coated arrow into the monster's front shoulder, hoping like hell Lucas didn't manage to move into the shot. The creature reared back and howled in pain, turning its glowing red eyes on Shane. Blood covered its sharp teeth and powerful, wide jaw, and Shane feared he was already too late. The grim's hesitation gave Shane the time he needed to reload, and this time, the crossbow bolt caught the grim between the eyes. The creature toppled over, covering Lucas in gore.

"Lucas!" Shane rushed forward, alert in case the grim had not hunted alone. Usually, they were solitary creatures, but nothing worked the way it used to, and Shane had learned the hard way not to take chances.

Lucas groaned, trapped beneath the body of the dead beast. Shane slung his crossbow over his shoulder on its strap and hefted the grim off of his partner. He couldn't tell how much of the blood was the grim's and how much was Lucas's.

"Got…shoulder," Lucas moaned.

Shane knelt beside him, triaging the wound. Lucas's shirt and jacket were ripped and bloody where the grim had sunk its teeth into the meat of his upper arm, and a swipe of the creature's claws had opened a set of gashes across his chest.

That's bad, Shane thought. He fought down panic and thought quickly, then shimmied out of his own coat long enough to strip off his flannel shirt and rip it into pieces.

Shane wadded up one section to stanch the flow of blood from the bite, then tied the wad in place with what had been a sleeve. He did the same for the chest wound.

"How bad?" Lucas managed.

"More than I can stitch up," Shane said. "We need to get you help."

"Not far to Green Farm." Lucas hated admitting pain, so the fact that he was panting gave Shane an idea of just how bad it was.

"Yeah. Far enough," Shane muttered. "Gonna have to get you to the farm. I'll get the bags, then we need to go."

He pulled Lucas to his feet as gently as he could and pretended he didn't see the tightness in his partner's face or hear the moan he bit back. Shane had a thinner, narrower build, while Lucas had always been more muscular. That made hauling his injured buddy all the harder, since Shane swore Lucas weighed a ton although, in reality, they were both lean from scant rations. Lucas stumbled beside him as Shane kept his gaze fixed on the motel. The trek seemed to take forever.

"I'll be back," Shane said as he eased Lucas into a plastic chair in the lobby. He grabbed their bedrolls and saddlebags, then went to the garage to fetch the horses, all the while expecting another grim to show up to finish the hunt.

Shane got the horses ready and then led them back, hoping Lucas remained conscious. When he returned to the lobby, his friend was pale and shaky, but still awake.

"Okay, you've got to stay with me," Shane cautioned. "Probably gonna hurt like hell. I'll drag this chair out beside Shadow, and then help you climb from the chair to the saddle."

"Fuck off," Lucas said, but the weakness in his voice took the heat from his comment. "I can get on my horse."

"Falling would be bad. And you're in no condition to

make decisions." Shane ignored Lucas's bravado, feeling vindicated when Lucas could barely keep his legs under him for the short distance between the lobby and the horses. Shane dragged the plastic chair along with them, then steadied Lucas and half-lifted him as he stepped up and swung his leg over the saddle.

"Do I need to tie you on?" It wouldn't be the first time they had ridden with one of them hurt.

"No. Just…fuck it hurts. Don't take the long way."

Shane hoped he had kept his worry out of his expression, but Lucas knew him too well to be fooled if he hadn't already figured out the danger for himself.

He fastened Shadow's reins to his own saddle, so Lucas only had to worry about keeping himself in the saddle. Not for the first time, he missed the convenience of GPS and the efficiency of ambulances and emergency rooms. *Hell, even a hospital would be an improvement,* he thought. But they were out in the country on the outskirts of Mercer, Pennsylvania, and the small rural hospitals had shut down long ago as the power failed and supplies ran out.

He came to a crossroads and debated which way to go. Both led to Green Farm, but Shane couldn't afford to find out that a damaged bridge or other obstacle blocked their path. Lucas still bled steadily from his injuries, and even the best care Shane might find in time would fall short of a trauma center.

It wasn't until he'd already made his decision, trusting his gut, and started down the road that Shane realized he'd followed the path where the faint song in his mind sang the loudest.

Green Farm lived up to its name. Before, it had been a cluster of Amish farms with a pie and produce stand along the state highway that ran along one side of the land. Now, it remained a farm, but it had also become an enclave, a sanctuary for those who needed somewhere to go when the world ended and were willing to adapt. The same old school ways that had often made the Amish the butt of jokes had been what ultimately saved them and held out hope that society could rebuild.

The palisade fence at Green Farm was new. It appeared to stretch around the perimeter of the enclave, and Shane guessed it had been built to protect the residents from creatures like the grim—and humans who were arguably worse.

"US Marshals Collins and Maddox, and my partner is bleeding, so we need to come in now," Shane snapped when two bearded young men in the plain clothing of the sect called down to him from a watchtower at the locked gates.

The two men exchanged a glance, then one ran to open the gate. Shane rode in, sparing a worried look behind him. Lucas had fallen silent soon after they had started on the road, and his ashen color and drawn expression made Shane even more worried than he had been before. In the old days, any emergency room probably could have handled the wounds. But that was Before. Now, resources were scarce to non-existent, or hellishly difficult to find if they hadn't vanished. This was the best he could do. Lucas wouldn't make it to the next depot.

"I'll run ahead and tell Doc you're coming," the second guard said, and took off toward where Shane vaguely remembered the doctor's house and office were located.

Dr. David Preston was waiting on his porch when Shane and Lucas rode up. He and the guard came forward to help

Shane get Lucas out of the saddle without falling. Lucas looked far too pale, and his skin felt cold.

"Got ambushed by a grim," Shane said as the three men carried Lucas inside. "I shot it, and Lucas did his best to fight it off, but there's a bite and some gashes. He's lost a lot of blood."

"Do you know his blood type?"

Shane rattled off the information. "And as it happens, we're the same type, so I can donate if you need me to." That had come in handy more than once over the years, in the Army as well as during their time as Marshals.

"Good to know. Let's see how it goes. Let's get him onto my table and see about cleaning the wounds. Those creatures' bites go sour easily. That's never been a good thing—but it's worse now."

Shane knew what Doc Preston meant. Antibiotics were scarce, and what might still be manufactured on a small, local scale could no longer be distributed like before. That put a premium on folk cures and old knowledge, as well as those whose medical knowledge combined with some healing magic.

"I'll take care of your horses," the guard volunteered, "if you want to get what you need from your packs." Shane thanked the man and grabbed a few essentials after the three of them got Lucas settled.

"Eat something," Preston said. "There's food in the kitchen. You'll need it if we have to do a transfusion. I'll yell if I need you."

Darkness had fallen on the ride to Green Farm. The whole way there, Shane feared that at any moment, a pack of grims—or something worse—would come lunging from the shadows and finish them both. In truth, he'd been expecting that for years, even Before. They'd come close so many times, in Afghanistan, and then as Marshals. Sooner or later, the time would come when fate decided it had been cheated long enough.

"But it will not be this day," Shane muttered to himself, quoting one of his favorite movies.

He tried to ignore the pang he always felt when he remembered. Watching those movies had grown much more difficult, and he might not see some ever again. In the old days, he and Lucas often passed the time in the car dueling nerd quotes, trying to out-geek the other. Their shared love of comics, video games, and superheroes had drawn them together in grade school and provided a life-long bond. Now it was bittersweet, an unspoken effort not to forget details from a world that had radically, permanently, changed.

The Amish had never relied on modern conveniences like electricity in their homes—although they did make a pragmatic exception for their barns and carpentry shops. That meant that their transition in the aftermath went far more smoothly. Shane made his way around Preston's kitchen by lantern light, hungry enough to be content with cheese and slices of thick, homemade bread with butter.

The door to Preston's office remained shut, and Shane tried to take it as a good sign that he hadn't been summoned. He pulled a dog-eared book from his pack, but he was too worried to read and too exhausted to pace. He stared at the book and realized that it was one of Lucas's fantasy novels. Shane tended toward sci-fi, but books were scarce, and he and Lucas always traded when they did find a stash of books in an abandoned house or not-completely-looted store.

He whistled to pass the time, cycling through as many of his classic rock favorites as he could remember. Shane rarely bothered to know the words. Lucas sang, another way they kept boredom at bay during all the long stake-outs and dreary car rides. Now, even whistling didn't quell his nervousness.

The wind-up clock on the mantle told him two hours had elapsed by the time Dr. Preston finally opened the door. Shane sprang to his feet. "Do you need me? Does Lucas need blood?"

Preston walked out, wearing a blood-spattered cloth apron. "He's going to be okay. You're welcome to go see him, but he's still under. Didn't need blood after all. Would have done a transfusion if we didn't have a choice, but I prefer not to if we can help it."

Shane felt himself relax for the first time since the attack. "Thank you."

Preston shrugged. "You're Marshals. We appreciate what you do for all of us. The folks here may not venture out much beyond our borders, but we do try to keep up with what goes on in the world."

Shane sighed. "You might want to rethink that, Doc. What goes on out there ain't so great."

"Was it ever?"

Shane's laugh was harsh. "A damned sight better than it is now, pardon my language."

"I've said worse when I tripped over something in the barn," Preston replied with a conspiratorial smile. "As for how it was Before—it's different for us. Our folks can't mourn what was never theirs. And yet, they would never wish what's happened on anyone."

"Maybe you had the right idea all along," Shane said with a sigh. "Keep it simple. Your folks still knew how to get by when everything went wrong." He paused. "Except…I didn't think the Amish went to school long enough to become a doctor."

Preston chuckled. "I didn't start out Amish. When the Events happened, I figured they had the most stable community, and I offered my services, in exchange for converting.

They probably wouldn't have taken me up on it Before, but… well, things are different now."

"That's an understatement."

"If you feel up to it, you and I could get Lucas into a bed and off my surgical table," Preston offered. "I've got a guest room for him, and I can make up the couch for you."

"I'd be grateful," Shane said, and now that the crisis was over, he felt exhaustion in every muscle. "And I'm willing to work for our room and board while he recovers. Wouldn't be the first time I've mucked out the barn."

Preston chuckled. "I'll take you up on that—tomorrow. Let's get you two settled before you fall over and I end up with two patients instead of one."

2

The next three weeks found a quiet rhythm. Despite Lucas's protests, Preston insisted that he stay and recover fully, saying that he would not clear a farm hand to go back to work from such an injury any sooner. Lucas grudgingly gave in, but he insisted on helping with light chores around the house and doctor's office to keep from going stir crazy. Shane tended their horses and helped in the barn, lending a hand for any farm work.

At night, he and Lucas played poker or one of the well-worn fantasy card games Shane kept in his duffle. It was another pastime carried over from long, boring weeks babysitting Mob witnesses in the old days, one that transitioned well now that power for electronics was hard to come by. Shane missed binge-watching horror movies and the all-night online gaming that used to fill empty evenings, but cards were a sociable substitute. Preston joined them now and again when his duties permitted.

"There you are," Preston said when Shane came back inside after an early morning in the barn. "Thought you'd want to know, Lucas is cleared to go. I know he's been champing at the bit for a while, but I wanted to make sure he healed up clean and solid before you two headed out. The road's no place to open up stitches or deal with an infection."

Shane wholeheartedly agreed, although he and Lucas had managed through some bad injuries plenty of times since the world fell apart. "I'm amazed he didn't meet me at the door with our bags packed," he replied with a chuckle.

"I haven't told him yet." Preston hesitated. "I know you have important work to do out there, but I'll be sorry to see you go," he admitted. "The stable hands will miss you, too. They say you've more than done your share."

Shane shrugged. "I like to keep busy. And helping on some of the carpentry was a nice change. My dad was in construction. Maybe it's in my blood a little."

He didn't mention that his parents and two brothers had died in the Events. Preston didn't ask. He didn't have to.

"If you ever decide to quit being Marshals, I'll put in a good word for you here," Preston joked.

"Stranger things have happened." Personally, Shane figured that he and Lucas would die with their boots on.

"Well, the offer stands," Preston replied, clapping him on the shoulder. "Go talk to Lucas and let me know what kind of provisions you'll need and when you want to get back on the road. We'll make sure you have what you need."

Shane thanked him and headed toward Lucas's room. He paused when he reached the door to the bedroom and ran a hand over his face. It had been too damn close. Shane still had nightmares about the attack. No one really knew what prowled in the night nowadays. Regular travelers wouldn't have had a chance. They'd only survived because they were ex-military, US Marshals, with all the training that entailed. And still, it had been a near thing.

He burst in without knocking and caught Lucas trying to pull his pants on. At the unexpected intrusion, Lucas wobbled and nearly toppled over with one leg stuck in his trousers.

"What the…fudge?" Lucas said, catching himself at the last minute and censoring his language out of respect for their host. "You ever hear of knocking?"

"Where's the fun in that?" Shane replied, grinning. "If you're well enough to walk, you're well enough for me to go back to irritating the crap out of you."

"Joy," Lucas replied in a droll tone. He regained his balance and pulled his pants up, giving a huff at the indignity. "A little privacy here? I'm trying to get dressed."

"Seriously?" Shane questioned, leaning against the wall. "They sent us into the bathroom together in elementary school since the time we were in third grade. Military barracks. Crappy hotels. And, we've been on the road for three years now. I'm long past needing to sneak up on you if I wanted to get an eyeful. You flatter yourself."

Lucas managed a smile that was almost like normal. "Yeah, yeah."

Shane closed the door and walked farther into the room, to sit on a wooden chair near the bed. Lucas picked up the pitcher next to the basin on a washstand and sluiced water over his face. In the two weeks they'd been here, stubble had become a full, dark beard, and his hair, which he also usually kept close-cut, had also grown longer.

"Guess I'm getting a head start on my winter beard." He sighed, looking in the mirror. Shane could see the toll the injury had taken on Lucas. He'd lost weight, and despite the enforced inactivity of recovery, he had dark circles under his eyes.

Shane and Lucas had been a team since they'd been picked for partners in third-grade dodgeball, and even the end of the world hadn't changed that. Shane was blond, with the kind of trustworthy good looks that made it far too easy for him to get what he wanted with a smile and a twinkle in his eye. Lucas had olive skin and black hair, and his moody vibe had been intimidating, even back in school, growing more so after a couple of tours of duty together and then joining the Marshals.

"Where've you been?" Lucas asked.

"Playing farmhand. Not sure I could ever get used to the suspenders and hats for myself, but Green Farm is a nice place."

"Your folks always did have a backyard garden," Lucas said, sitting down to pull on his boots. "And my dad went deer hunting. That's about as country as we ever got."

"Back when there were cities."

"Yeah." Lucas's parents, sister, and brother hadn't survived the Events.

"I let you sleep and went and sat on the porch. Thank God the Amish believe in coffee," Shane replied. "Talked to the doc. He thinks you're ready to go back on the road."

Lucas seemed to take stock of himself in the mirror, sighed in frustration, and headed back toward the bed. "I'm ready to be gone," he said, pulling his shirt over the newly healed scars on his chest and shoulder.

"Kinda nice to be somewhere for a while where nothing's trying to kill us," Shane replied.

Lucas snorted. "If we stick around long enough, you'll manage to annoy the fu…dge out of them. They'll probably chase us off with axes and scythes."

"I'm the people person, remember?" It was an old sparring match, almost as old as the debate over which of them was taller. Shane stood half an inch taller than Lucas, a point his friend would never concede.

"Says you," Lucas retorted. He stretched, then grimaced as

the newly healed skin protested. "Ouch. I remember when we just transported WITSEC informants, chased down some fugitives, and only had to worry about the Mob," Lucas said wistfully. "Good times."

When the cities went dark, and the relentless bustle of cars, trains, and planes came to an abrupt halt, creatures that had awaited their turn to take back the night slunk from their hiding places to remind humankind that they were no longer the apex predators.

"But still, it feels wrong not to keep moving," Lucas went on. "Places to go, people to see, things to kill." Shane knew that Lucas had never been able to sit still.

"Messes to clean up," Shane added.

Back in school, they'd called Lucas's jitters ADHD and given him pills. The Army liked the hyper-vigilant focus the pills gave Lucas, a good thing for a sniper. But since the Events, the pills, like much of the Army, were long gone. Shane was resigned to Lucas just being twitchy as fuck. It suited Lucas as if he'd reverted to his natural state, like most everything else had.

A knock at the door startled them, although Shane knew they were safe here.

"See? Someone knows how to knock," Lucas muttered. "Come in!" he said in a louder voice.

Doc Preston walked in and cast an assessing gaze over Lucas. "You're up. I told Shane you're healed enough to go back on the road. I'd be most displeased if all my handiwork on those stitches was for naught." One hundred careful stitches, which would leave a scar. Shane had already taken to calling Lucas "quilt boy" when he was out of arm's reach.

"Have your folks heard anything about what's going on out there?" Shane asked.

"Look at it this way—we've already had the apocalypse, so nothing else is too bad by comparison, right?" Preston replied. "Heard there've been floods to the northeast, and wildfires in the west. The usual."

The end of the world, when it came, wasn't due to just one thing—it was a cascade of one calamity after another. Some people referred to the year-long shit storm that had torn apart modern civilization as "The Cataclysm," but most people just called it "The Events."

"Good to know," Lucas said. "Not that it changes the circuit we ride. When we can, we try to pitch in and lend a hand when that shi—stuff happens."

"I imagine there's too much territory, and not enough of you Marshals to go around," Preston replied. He didn't know the half of it, Shane thought. *And that lets him sleep at night, so we're not going to tell him.*

The aftermath of the Events had badly strained the military and law enforcement, and without modern communication and transportation, they were stretched even thinner. Shane and Lucas were the only Marshals in their area, which covered parts of Ohio, Pennsylvania, and West Virginia. Too much space, too many problems, for just two men, but they did the best they could.

Shane and Lucas made the rounds, thanking the many people who had brought food, tended their horses, or stopped by with well-wishes. And of course, there was Preston, who had taken them into his home and saved Lucas's life.

"Come back, when the circuit brings you this way," Preston said, walking with them and their horses to the front gate of the enclave. "Bring us news. But try to come back in one piece."

They shook his hand. "Deal," Lucas said, an empty

promise but a pleasant thought. They swung up into the saddles and rode out, and Shane had to admit that he was happy to be back on the road.

"I think the horses figured they had a vacation," Shane said, riding next to Lucas. Route 19 was the most direct way south other than the interstate, but they didn't expect to see a lot of fellow travelers.

Once in a while, peddlers or a trader caravan wended their way across the broken landscape, but that was more likely in summer, not now, when fall storms were in the offing. Most folks stayed close to home unless a disaster forced them to relocate. Shane thought it was as if Fate picked up the snow globe of the world and shook it, just for the hell of it, to see where the pieces would land.

The land on either side of them had been farmland or pastures for horses and cows. A few small hamlets at the crossroads had offered gas, convenience stores, and beer. Most of that was gone now. Violent storms had chased off some residents, while the collapse of big parts of the power grid had shuttered most businesses. The ones who remained survived by banding together into communities every bit as tightly knit as the Amish and toughing it out, helping each other through fire, flood, and famine. Unlike the Amish, some of those enclaves were decidedly unfriendly to outsiders, even Marshals.

Just north of I-80, Shane saw two travelers coming toward them. Their clothing made identification easy and immediate.

"Looks like a couple of the IT Priests are heading our way," he said to Lucas.

The two riders were dressed in black academic robes. Each wore several strands of Mardi Gras beads, from which hung a fandom pendant. In this case, the dark-haired young man on the left had a Transformer medallion, while his companion, a fine-featured blond whose gender Shane couldn't guess, wore a Decepticon amulet.

"Greetings, Marshals!" the dark-haired man said, noting the badges Shane and Lucas wore, prominently displayed. "I'm Brother Jon, and this is Devon."

"Hello, monks. What brings you this way?" Lucas asked.

"Heading to the Thiel campus," the blond replied. "We've just made a circuit of the towers and nodes. We'll rest a bit and get new orders, then head out again."

When the Events destroyed cities, unleashed outbreaks, and sent the survivors fleeing, many college students realized they couldn't go home. The universities realized that with their own power plants and extensive facilities, they could function as independent villages. Sporting fields were plowed and planted for food, flax, and cotton, and escaped livestock from abandoned farms got corralled and brought within the palisade fencing that sprang up to protect the inhabitants.

Townsfolks who didn't flee either moved on campus or took shelter there during the new, unpredictable storms. Students suddenly found their majors had become their professions and pitched in. ROTC and sporting teams were deputized to campus security and local law enforcement or helped with the farming. But the engineering and computer science majors and their professors found a whole new calling.

The whole "priesthood" thing had started as a joke, gallows humor after the Events, a self-deprecating nod to the stereotype that programmers didn't have a social life and didn't get laid, and that college students with loans might as well have taken a vow of poverty. But when universities realized that they and the few remaining scattered government facilities were the last guardians of what remained of the internet, the task of keeping the backbone of the system functioning became an urgent way to save knowledge and preserve a key communications tool.

And so engineers and programmers teamed up to ride circuits between campuses, doing their best to keep what remained of the system and its servers functioning. No one knew who came up with the idea of the robes, beads, and geek symbols, but it immediately identified the wearers to all who saw them and afforded some protection from brigands.

"Any news from the road?" Shane asked. "We were sidelined for a bit from an injury."

"We came across I-80," Devon said. "Didn't have any trouble, but we've heard there have been some incidents on the side roads."

"Incidents?" Lucas asked, immediately going into what Shane thought of as "cop mode."

Jon nodded. "Brigands, robbing peddlers and stealing horses."

"Where?" Lucas pressed.

"Around the state game lands, just south of here," Devon replied. "That's all we know."

Shane and Lucas exchanged a glance. "All right. We'll look into it," Shane assured the monks.

"We have a message for you," Jon said. "Professor Gibbons at Slippery Rock has us all looking for you two."

"What's going on?" Lucas asked.

"We're losing contact with IOT."

"Eye-aught?" Shane echoed, confused.

"I-O-T. Internet of Things," Devon replied. "You probably never noticed, before everything went to hell in a handbasket, that all the equipment and appliances around you were networked to the internet. So your coffee maker and your refrigerator and your smart TV could all report back to their manufacturers for software updates—and data mining."

"I think everyone's warranty is fucked, at this point," Lucas pointed out.

"Not the point," Jon said. "We were able to hack into the IOT early on, and we used the reports to get data. Anything on batteries or with a generator—or in the places where the grid isn't down, still has power—became our eyes and ears. That's what helped us feed you the intel you needed to know the safe routes out of the D.C. suburbs and helped the responders on the coast get around where the bridges were out and the roads were flooded."

"So Big Brother actually served a purpose," Lucas snarked. "And now you're losing contact? Why? Grid going dark? Batteries running low?"

"That's some of it, but I'm afraid there's more," Devon said. "We think something is actively trying to block the signal in places."

"You're sure it's not just a glitch?" Shane asked, frowning.

Jon shook his head. "No. Something's cut off the signal in certain areas. We haven't figured out a pattern, but the signal isn't failing—it's being blocked. We don't know what that means, or what could do that—or why anyone would want to."

"Could it be something natural?" Lucas wondered aloud. "Weird, but natural? We've had more than our share of that kind of thing, lately."

"Maybe," Devon allowed. "We're looking into it, and we've got queries out to the other priests, but no one's given us anything usable yet."

"All right," Shane replied. "Keep us posted. What else?"

"We've completely lost touch with the enclave at Site R," Jon said gravely. "We've accepted the probability that they've been wiped out."

3

"What the fuck is Site R?" Lucas asked. "And why should I care? Boston and Philadelphia are gone, too. We deal with it."

Jon gave him a long-suffering look. "Neither Boston nor Philadelphia were secure location bunkers for top government officials. Site R—Raven Rock—was. Very hush-hush. That location was built to withstand everything up to and including a nuclear bomb to the East Coast."

"So if it's gone dark..." Shane said.

Devon nodded. "Yeah. Gettysburg University alerted us a week ago. They've been trying to reach Site R and lost contact. So they put out a call for anyone who heard from the Marshals to send you their way and see what's going wrong. You'll probably want to swing through and talk to the Gettysburg folks, then head south from there."

"Okay," Lucas said. "We'll head that way."

"Travel safely," Devon said. "May the Force be with you, and all that jazz."

"And also with you," Lucas added with a smirk, riffing on his Catholic upbringing.

"May the odds be ever in your favor," Shane returned. Lucas knew that since the Events, both he and Shane had lost faith in a god that seemed to have left without a forwarding address. That left them to find comfort in other things, like the books and movies that they didn't want to forget.

Lucas and Shane said nothing until after Jon and Devon had ridden off. Finally, Lucas turned to his partner. "So...Site R?"

Shane shrugged. "Might as well have a look. We were going south anyhow—now we've got a destination." While their circuit took them through the territory on a regular basis, they often changed their route when an incident required their attention.

They had ridden for about an hour when Lucas came to an abrupt halt and waved silently for Shane to stop as well. Two ghosts stood in the middle of the highway, spirits Lucas could see but Shane could not.

"Ghosts?" Shane asked quietly, guessing from Lucas's reaction.

Lucas nodded. He'd always been able to see ghosts, but Before, the appearances had been rare, usually only in dire moments. For obvious reasons, that ability wasn't one he publicized to his colleagues or superiors as a US Marshal, although Shane had known about Lucas's "gift" since they were children.

One of the spirits that blocked their way was a middle-aged man. The other was a teenage boy. Both bore the head wounds that had killed them. The ghosts stood in the middle of the highway, but Lucas felt no threat. Instead, their gestures and worried expressions conveyed a warning.

"Those brigands Jon and Devon mentioned? I think they might be up ahead."

"We're close to the state game lands," Shane replied. "You

think it's Dan Metheney's preppers, the guys we ran into before?"

Lucas nodded. "Yeah. They were the first ones who came to mind."

When everything fell apart, the natural cooperation that fostered civilization's rise showed itself more often than reality TV had predicted. People banded together to evacuate after floods and wildfires, forming convoys to reach safer locations, working together to rebuild. Lucas and Shane were on the front lines and had been impressed and surprised time and again when people had shown their better natures.

But some didn't. Groups that had been suspicious and protective before the Event grew even more defensive and insular. Those who had long predicted the end of modern civilization had almost been elated to have their warnings prove true, although no one had really foreseen the way the end happened when it came.

Those groups focused on protecting their territory, sure that everyone meant to take what they had stored up. Lucas noticed these groups didn't seem to mind taking what others had.

Dan Metheney's group had caused problems long before the Event. Metheney headed up a group of local bad boys who had rap sheets as long as their arms, on everything from arson to assault. Authorities had been busting them since their high school days, but nothing ever seemed to stick that was serious enough to send them away for long, or make them leave the area. When everything fell apart, Metheney and his followers turned cultish. More than once, Lucas and Shane had to intervene.

Now, if they were waylaying travelers and, even worse, killing them, the Marshals had no choice but to put a stop to the problem. Lucas, in particular, had very little patience with Metheney's preppers.

"I thought they'd be smart enough not to cause problems again, after what happened last time."

"Yeah, well. Guess they're not as smart as you thought they were." Six months ago, Lucas and Shane had caught men from the preppers enclave who were harassing other enclaves and trying to steal from nearby towns that weren't abandoned. The two Marshals had given the men a beat-down they should have remembered and returned them to the prepper compound with a stern warning to the leaders. A warning that obviously hadn't been taken to heart.

"How do you want to do this?" Shane asked.

Lucas considered the options. He expected to be outnumbered, but he didn't know by how many. The preppers had stockpiled everything they expected to need after a crash, which most certainly included ammunition. And unlike Lucas and Shane, who had to carefully conserve their scarce bullets while traveling hundreds of miles through dangerous territory, the preppers rarely had to defend their compound against real threats. That meant they would also likely be outgunned.

In the old days, carjacking or highway crimes would have been the responsibility of other branches of law enforcement. Now, Shane and Lucas were often the only representatives in their territory, like the sheriffs of the Old West. And aside from the local authorities that survived in small towns and enclaves, the two Marshals were also the only remaining vestige of a larger government that had, for all practical purposes, utterly collapsed.

"I think we need to see what we're dealing with," Lucas replied. "And be ready to put a stop to it—permanently."

They tied up their horses in a small grove just off the road where their mounts would be hidden from view. Lucas and

Shane took a variety of weapons—crossbows, swords, and shotguns—since they didn't know how many of the brigands they might be facing. Then they split up, one on each side of the road, moving stealthily through the scrub brush.

The ghosts' warning had stopped them just a mile from where an improvised roadblock of tree trunks and wooden crates barricaded both lanes of traffic. The brigands sat around a campfire in front of canvas tents, a camp that looked like it had been in place for a while and was intended to last for a while.

Lucas couldn't see Shane, but the teenage boy's ghost gave him an idea of where his partner was in the underbrush. The older man guided Lucas, bringing him to a spot behind the camp where recently disturbed ground revealed several shallow graves.

"Fuck," Lucas muttered. He had debated how to deal with the robbers, but proof that they were killing travelers made the decision for him. They needed to be stopped—and the prepper compound needed to be sent a message.

He crept closer and got his first look at the killers. They wore camouflage fatigues, although Lucas doubted any of them had ever been in the military. Four men, three of whom who looked to be barely in their twenties, and an older guy, their leader, probably in his forties. The men had buzzed haircuts, muscular builds that likely owed a nod to 'roids, and a cockiness that immediately set Lucas's teeth on edge.

"Been too quiet," one of the men said. A jug of what Lucas guessed was some kind of home brew sat beside his dented lawn chair.

"Maybe it's time to change locations," another man said, reaching for the jug. "Maybe word got out."

"How?" The older man gave the speaker a look. "There wasn't anyone left to tell the tale." The others chuckled, and Lucas felt anger tighten his gut. The group of four men had eight horses, giving Lucas to suspect they had killed at least four travelers, perhaps more if any had been on foot. A haphazard pile of knapsacks, duffel bags, and other belongings beside one of the tents suggested the spoils.

In the old days, Lucas abided by due process. Now, he had two ghosts' bearing witness to their murders, and evidence of more crimes. In the rough justice that survived, that was enough. Shane was waiting on him, willing to follow his lead. Lucas decided it was time to end the problem.

He fired once with the crossbow, putting a bolt through the neck of the leader. The man fell clutching at the quarrel, a look of shock on his face. Before the others could react, Lucas followed that up with a blast from his shotgun, catching the nearest man in the torso. A second later, Shane's arrow took the third man through the chest. The last of the men looked around wildly.

"Ken? Billy? Oh, God. Jason? Oh, my god," the fourth man cried out, panicking. Any sympathy Lucas had for him had vanished when he'd seen the shallow graves.

Shane's shotgun blast hit its target, and the last of the brigands collapsed in a bloody pile atop his fellow robbers.

Lucas waited before showing himself, in case the robbers had friends who might come in response to the attack. But after a few minutes, he decided the four men had been on their own.

A glance at the pitiful stash next to the tent made Lucas furious. He'd already made up his mind as Shane came out of concealment and jogged to meet him.

"Go cut saplings," Lucas snapped as he drew his sword.

Shane cocked his head, trying to figure out what Lucas had planned. "Lucas—"

"I'm going to make sure everyone knows what happens to highwaymen," Lucas replied in a tight voice.

"The preppers probably have AKs," Shane said. "Think about this carefully."

"That's the only reason I'm not planning to march up to their gates," Lucas said in a tight voice. "Go."

Shane walked away, but he was still close enough to cringe at the sound as Lucas brought his sword down and severed the leader's head. When he finished with the others, he left the bodies where they lay and went to break down the roadblock. Shane returned after a while with four sturdy saplings, whittled to have sharp points on either end.

"Pretty sure there's nothing in the rules about leaving the heads of your enemies on pikes," Shane said as Lucas stuck the first shaft into the ground beside the tent.

"Pretty sure the rules were written when there were more than two Marshals for three whole fuckin' states." Lucas couldn't hide his anger, and he knew Shane understood the frustration of not having caught the killers earlier, not being able to be everywhere at once, to protect the people who had already lived through the collapse of their world.

"I'll sink the pikes. You can deal with the heads," Shane said, wrinkling his nose in disgust. It wasn't just the gore, Lucas knew. They had field dressed enough deer in the last three years. But they both knew this was different, that the predators they had killed had still been human, no matter how twisted. And the fact that they'd come to this was just more proof of how far the world had fallen, and them with it.

Lucas slung the bodies over the dead men's horses, tying them onto the saddles. Then he sent the horses galloping with a smack to the rump, shouting and waving his arms to make sure they headed back where they came from. Afterward, he and Shane cleaned up as best they could using a few cast-off shirts.

"What about the stuff?" Shane asked with a nod toward the robbers' loot and the raiders' campsite.

"Leave it. Someone will make use of it," Lucas said, not wanting anything that belonged to either the killers or their victims. He saw enough ghosts as it was.

"You saw something, with your Gift, didn't you?" Lucas asked with a glance at his partner, who had gone along with their plan more readily than Lucas expected. Not that Shane wouldn't have agreed in the end, but Lucas knew that his partner still clung to a desire for something better than the rough-and-ready frontier justice that sufficed after the end of the world as they once knew it.

Shane nodded. "I…had a vision. I saw how they died. They begged for their lives. Offered to ride away and never tell anyone. Ken, the leader, still killed them." His expression grew hard. "They deserved what we gave them, and more."

"Fuck, yeah. You should be proud of me. I really want to ride over to their compound and go Waco on their asses."

Shane gave a bitter chuckle. "They've got AKs, Lucas. AR-15s. Hell, probably grenade launchers and bazookas. If they didn't already own an armory before things went to hell, they probably bought or stole enough weapons afterward to hold off a whole fuckin' platoon." He looked at the blood-soaked ground and the heads on pikes like ghoulish road signs. "I think you've made your point."

Shane didn't see ghosts, but Lucas did. The older man and the teenage boy were joined by six more ghosts, and Lucas had a feeling they were not all of Ken's victims, just the ones who hadn't moved on. The man's ghost took in the savage message of the heads on pikes, and looked saddened, but not outraged. His gaze shifted to Lucas, and then he nodded in acknowledgment. In the next breath, the ghosts faded from view.

"I think the ghosts are at peace now," Lucas said, knowing that Shane would have guessed why he seemed to be staring into space. "I think some of them couldn't move on until the killing stopped, and a few of them were trying to warn people off."

"I hope you're right," Shane said as they walked back to their horses. "They've been through enough." He left it unsaid that the same was true for all of them.

4

"What?" Lucas asked. "You've been distracted since we left the ghosts behind. You haven't said a word for hours."

"Nothing. It's just—" Shane started, then stopped speaking and shook his head.

"What?"

Shane looked away, uncomfortable. "I keep hearing songs in my head."

"Good thing, because the radio doesn't work anymore."

Shane gave him the stink eye. "Not funny. It's different. The song isn't a regular song. Not like something I heard and remembered. More like birds or whales or..." He let his voice drift off. "It's hard to explain."

Lucas frowned. "You think it has something to do with your visions?"

"Don't know. It changes. Sometimes it's soothing. Other times, I could swear it's agitated, like it's trying to warn me." He finally turned to Lucas. "Right before we split up to track the preppers, it got very... jittery. Discordant."

"I didn't used to be able to see ghosts as much. Maybe

you're growing into a new part of your abilities," Lucas replied. He could see that Shane felt uncomfortable admitting the oddity. "Hell, you've seen what the world is like now. Ghosts. Monsters. Shifters. Vamps. So is it possible your psychic hotline is picking up on a new frequency? Why not?"

Shane managed a slight smile that looked both grateful and self-conscious. "Thanks. I'm still trying to figure it out, but I don't think ignoring it is an option."

"Have you found a pattern?" Lucas asked.

"I notice it more when we're around park land and less when we're in towns or cities. But that might just be because there's less to distract me."

They headed south, stopping when Lucas spotted a small pond where they could clean up and wash the blood away. The farther they went, the darker the sky became as heavy gray clouds began to roll in.

"Looks like we've got something coming in from the northwest," Lucas noted, pointing to where the clouds were darkest.

"Think we can make it to Cooper's Lake? I don't really want to get soaked and sleep rough."

Lucas eyed the storm clouds. "Maybe. It's been moving in quickly. Pick up the pace, we might make it."

The horses didn't seem to mind, and Lucas wondered if they, too, could sense the coming rain. The temperature had dropped since they set out that morning, and the wind started to blow. Shane had grown quiet, and Lucas saw him put fingers to his temple.

"Headache?"

Shane nodded. "Yeah. But…it's the song again. It went away for a while, after the preppers. But the farther south we go, the louder it gets. And…it's different. I don't know whether that means it's coming from somewhere else or it has a new meaning. Or…maybe I'm just imagining the whole thing."

Lucas doubted that, given how uncomfortable Shane looked. They'd known each other all their lives, and Lucas had never seen Shane exaggerate or make up symptoms, not even to get out of the worst duties. Shane had always had a bit of the Sight about him, even before the Events brought his gift to the fore. Lucas had always trusted his own intuition, and with all the changes the Events had wrought, he'd come to accept that the world had become a different place and that the rules were permanently different.

Two miles out from Cooper's Lake, Lucas knew they were in trouble. The wind had grown strong enough to lash their clothing, and the cold rain felt like needles. Their horses moved faster on their own accord. Lucas had glimpsed several ghosts along the road, and those that appeared to be more than faded remnants gestured in warning for the travelers to find shelter.

"The song is practically screaming in my head," Shane yelled above the rain. "We've got to get off the road. It's going to be bad."

Just then, the wail of an air raid siren cut through the howl of the wind. Lucas knew that some communities had dug their antique manual sirens out of basements and museums when the grid went down. The sound sent a chill down his spine.

"Ride for it!" he shouted, digging his heels into Shadow's ribs. The stallion needed no further urging, and lunged forward, with Shane and Red close behind.

They reached the gates of the Cooper's Lake stockade, drenched and shivering as the wind howled and the siren caterwauled. The sky overhead had turned a greenish black, and gusts were strong enough to rock them in their saddles.

"US Marshals, asking for sanctuary," Lucas said, fighting

his chattering teeth, as he fished out his badge for the sentry. The man looked equally miserable in his leather cape and broad-brimmed hat.

"I need permission from the king—"

"Tell King Kevin that Lucas and Shane are here. Hurry, before we die."

Moments later, the stockade's gate opened to let them in, and they rode into the Kingdom of Butler Highlands.

For decades, the Organization of Historic Interpreters, a large group of medieval re-enactors, had camped each summer at Cooper's Lake. They took great pride in preserving old ways of cooking, making clothing, spinning cloth, forging steel—pretty much all the day-to-day tasks of a medieval household. The more adventurous donned home-made armor and fought mock battles. That knowledge and the skills they honed came in handy when the modern world suddenly stopped working.

The flags of the kingdom flapped wildly, nearly tearing from their posts. Since the Events, the kingdom had expanded, taking up the entire five-hundred-acre campground. A wooden stockade fence ran the perimeter of the grounds. Permanent homes made of stone, daub, and wattle, scavenged bricks, and wood replaced the tents popular when the gathering was just for fun. Some of the dwellings had even been dug into the hillsides. Like the Amish, the residents of the kingdom chose to live with the limited technology of a long-ago era, accepting a lack of electricity and internet and going on about their lives.

The captain of the guards came running toward them. "Marshals. Welcome. His Majesty will want to see you. I'll take you there myself." He glanced at their mounts. "And of course, we'll provide food and water for your horses. Leave them with my men, and they'll be cared for."

Lucas and Shane left their horses and followed their

escort toward the unassuming building that served as the palace. It looked more like a bunker, made of cement block, painted white, with square towers on either end that served as watch posts. Flags and banners were the only adornments, besides a mural on the entry walls that showed what the gathering at Cooper's Lake had looked like Before.

A glorious mismatch of furnishings of all styles and colors filled the public rooms of the large, one-story building. The palace housed a courtroom, a council chamber, a few offices, the king's small apartment, and a large gathering room.

Kevin Henderson had been a tenured history professor in medieval studies Before. He'd been a long-time member of the Organization of Historic Interpretation, and one of the local group's leaders. Between his even temperament and his somewhat encyclopedic knowledge of how rulers had governed—for better and worse—Kevin had been elected king, by unanimous vote.

Now, the King of Butler Highlands looked more like a harried disaster relief organizer than a monarch. He wore a loose tunic over a pair of khaki pants and work boots. Collar-length, graying dark hair was mussed, as if he'd run his hands through it in frustration. He pushed his gold wire-rimmed glasses up his nose as he spoke to the people gathered around him, who were ready to head out into the storm.

"Make sure the people in more fragile housing come to the palace or go into the tunnels," Kevin ordered. "And the others need to shelter in place. Clear the open areas. Close the storm shutters. Consider it an emergency."

"How can we help, Your Majesty?" Lucas asked.

Kevin looked relieved at their offer. "Shane and Lucas—I can't say that I'm sorry the storm brought you to us. We'll need all the help we can get. Go with the guards. Get people to safety. We've always got folks who don't want to believe the warnings."

The wind drove the rain sideways. Bells clanged and sirens screamed in warning, loud enough to be heard over the storm. Lucas and Shane darted through the rain, soaked to the skin, to escort stragglers to shelter.

Lucas had to lean against the wind to keep moving, at enough of an angle that if the storm stopped suddenly, he would have fallen flat on his face. It reminded him of the time he and Shane had ridden out a hurricane in Miami when they were babysitting a key witness in a drug cartel case.

Only then, they'd been on the coast, where storms like this were normal. But increasingly violent storms were part of the domino effect of the Events, one disaster creating another. And the first, initial Cataclysm had wiped out FEMA and the communication and power grid, so surviving relief efforts were quickly overwhelmed. Since then, every area had been on its own to face increasingly volatile weather.

The wind snapped a tall wooden tent support with a crack like gunfire, and Lucas flinched. He and Shane trod through rapidly rising water toward a mother and two children who were soaked to the skin and struggling against the wind. Lucas took the children—one on his back and one in his arms—while Shane wrapped an arm around the woman's waist to keep her on her feet as they guided them to shelter. As soon as they handed off the family, they headed back outside.

Rain fell in gray sheets, and hail clattered on rooftops as the temperature fell. Across the compound, Lucas saw men struggling to get horses, donkeys, and cows into barns, while others attempted to herd the sheep and goats.

Before the Events, when Cooper's Lake was a summer

campground, and the Organization held a two-week re-enactment, most of the participants lived in big canvas tents, making the grounds look like a scene from a medieval movie drama. When the kingdom became a permanent enclave, the re-enactors worked together to gradually replace the tents and portable shelters with more solid buildings.

The storm was testing the strength of the enclave's construction. Lucas knew that anything built after the Events was strictly do-it-yourself, without inspectors or building codes, or professional crews. If the wind and hail didn't do damage, the rush of flood water as the storm gullies swelled past capacity was likely to strain even well-built dwellings.

"Shit!" Lucas cried out, flinching as a wooden house groaned and then collapsed.

"You think anyone's in there?" Shane yelled over the howling wind.

"We'd better check." Lucas struggled against the wind, with Shane right behind him. He had to walk at an angle to stay on his feet, and the rain lashed his skin, as bits of hail stung where they hit.

He and Shane fought their way toward the wreckage, and Lucas heard a thin wail, barely audible above the wind.

"I heard something!" he yelled to Shane. They waded into the wreckage, shouting to let survivors know they were nearby. A woman's scream cut through the storm, guiding Lucas and Shane toward a front room. They began to dig, throwing broken boards and splintered supports out of the way, until they could make out a shape beneath the wreckage. Part of a wall had fallen, with debris on top, but Lucas figured that they might be able to lift a section of a wooden door to get to the people trapped underneath.

"We can't clear all of this away—the pieces are too big," Shane warned.

Lucas nodded. "Okay. You hold up this end of the door,

and I'll go under to get them out." He sized up the opening, hoping he could fit through and make an escape passage. Shane put his back and shoulders into lifting up a section of debris, and Lucas crouched down to fit underneath. He spotted a woman and a small child huddled next to a desk that had kept the wall from crushing them but had also blocked their escape.

"Come with me." Lucas held out his hand.

A boy who looked to be about seven years old scrambled past him, and Lucas grabbed the woman's arm. "Are you hurt?" he asked. She shook her head. "Then come on. We don't have much time."

At first, he feared that she might have been pinned by other debris, but then she got on her hands and knees and crawled toward him.

"Hurry up!" Shane shouted. "I can't hold this much longer!"

Lucas grabbed the woman's wrist and pulled her to him, wrapping himself around her as he hustled her out. Just after they cleared the wreckage, Shane let go, and the door slammed down with a crash.

"Come on," Lucas said, holding on to the woman and child tightly. "We need to get you to shelter."

By the time they reached the palace, the public areas and gathering room were filled with frightened, rain-soaked people huddling together by the fireplace. Kevin was in the midst of the chaos, directing kitchen workers to dole out portions of soup and other volunteers to distribute blankets.

"Is this everyone?" Lucas asked dubiously. The room was full, but not crowded enough to account for all the residents of the kingdom.

King Kevin shook his head. "No. Just the ones whose houses might not stand up to the storm. The others stayed where they were, and some went down below, into the bunker that connects to the old mine tunnels." He sighed. "There've been two casualties, both hit with flying debris. I really miss the old days, when storms weren't usually life or death situations."

"What can we do?" Shane asked.

Kevin chuckled. "Nothing much left to do except try to make them comfortable and ride out the storm," he said. "I apologize, but I had to give away the guest room. Mine, too. So we'll all just have to find a nice spot on the floor for the night."

Lucas and Shane pitched in, helping to reunite families that had been separated by the storm, or giving a hand as volunteers passed out blankets and cold provisions, while the storm raged outside. Children cried, and adults talked in hushed tones.

Finally, when there was nothing else to be done, Lucas and Shane found an empty spot in the back hallway and sank to the floor with their backs to the wall.

"You know, I don't think I could do it," Lucas said. "Live like the Amish at Green Farm or the folks here. It's one thing to go without the conveniences because we have to, because the system broke. But if I could have them back again—"

"I'd take it in a New York minute," Shane agreed. "But then again, you didn't exactly enjoy roughing it, even when we were deployed."

"You have a job, you do it. But man, some of those guys—like Wisnewski, remember him? I swear he wanted to get in touch with his inner caveman. He was actually *disappointed* when we went back to base."

"He's probably doing just fine now," Shane replied. "Or, he got what he thought he could handle but couldn't, and he's holed up crying in the corner somewhere, losing his shit."

They were silent for a few moments. "What do you think about this Raven Rock 'Site R' stuff?" Lucas asked.

Shane shrugged. "Sounds suspicious for them to just go dark. I think we should look into it. But it might not end up being anything unusual. They could have gotten sick and died out. Or something might have gone wrong with the bunker, and they had to leave. All those things have happened to other groups."

"It just seems strange, in a location like that," Lucas mused. "I mean, if it was intended as a safe haven for the D.C. brass, you'd think it would have medical facilities and all the best supplies."

"There's enough weird stuff going on, I don't think anyone could have anticipated everything that could happen," Shane replied. "The weather's never acted like this since people started keeping records. Places that didn't use to get earthquakes get them now. And some of the diseases that mutated…"

"I get the point." Lucas didn't like to think about the changes more than the job required, which was far beyond what he sometimes thought his sanity could handle.

Were we the lucky ones to survive this long? Maybe the truly lucky got a fast death, instead of a slow one. Lucas tried to shift his thoughts away from the shadows that haunted his dreams. They had a job to do, a purpose that mattered. And considering how many people had lost everyone they cared about to the apocalypse, Lucas counted himself damn fortunate to still have Shane fighting beside him.

"You know, this isn't the worst place we've ridden out a storm," Lucas said, his voice thick with exhaustion.

"Definitely not," Shane replied. Lucas knew his partner remembered all too well taking refuge in caves, basements, and abandoned buildings that even the rats had deserted, back in the early days right after the Events.

Lucas's stitches ached, he felt their ride in every muscle, and he'd twisted his back getting the woman and her child to safety. His clothing was still damp enough to chafe. *Thank fuck for wool—still holds warmth.* Lucas let his head fall back, making himself as comfortable as he could and fell asleep before he could complain about Shane's snoring.

In his dreams, Lucas saw the hotel room of the Holiday Inn Express near Youngstown where he and Shane were holed up for the night with the witness they were escorting. They'd pulled over in a snowstorm bad enough that Lucas didn't want to push his luck, even with the four-wheel drive on their Chevy Suburban SUV.

The room was comfortable, in a practical, no-frills sort of way. They'd gone to a drive-through before the storm got too bad and raided the snacks at the hotel's small convenience store before they hunkered down for the night. Two beds, one for the witness, and one that Lucas and Shane would take turns sleeping in while the other stood watch.

He'd turned on the TV while they ate, too tired from driving to flip channels away from the news station that came on automatically. Lucas remembered that he was eating a bag of barbecued potato chips when everything changed.

Their government-issued, secure cell phones both went off with an emergency signal at the same time. Shane and Lucas exchanged a worried look, reaching for their phones in unison.

"Washington is under attack. Do not come in. Repeat, do not come in. Find a secure location outside of a city center and await further instructions."

"Oh my God!" Vinnie Scarpelli, their witness, pointed at the TV screen, pale as a dead fish. Lucas and Shane turned to watch footage of buildings crumbling in the nation's capital, as the bombs went off…

Lucas jerked awake, sweating and heaving for breath, disoriented for a moment until he remembered where he was. He closed his eyes and took a deep breath, trying to block out the ache that the dream always brought, the longing for a normality they had taken for granted and would never have again. No matter how often the dreams came, snippets of his life Before, the feeling of loss never dimmed.

The big room was dark, filled with the sound of steady breathing and the smell of wet clothing. Outside, the storm still roared, battering the cement-block building with hail that sounded like gunfire as it pelted the roof.

Shane's troubled murmurs roused Lucas, and he looked toward where his friend sat beside him, twitching in a restless sleep. Shane's deep frown and his worried tone told Lucas his partner's dreams were uneasy.

"Hey," he said quietly, bumping Shane's shoulder. "Wake up."

Shane didn't wake, and he kept on mumbling, growing more agitated. Lucas moved to crouch in front of him and took Shane by the shoulders, shaking him gently. "Come on. Wake up."

Shane woke with a gasp, like a swimmer rising out of the water and nearly out of air. "What?" he asked, not quite awake.

"You had a bad dream. So did I. But you were mumbling, and it didn't look like fun."

Shane shook his head as if he were trying to clear water from his ears. "I just...it wasn't a dream."

"Another vision," Lucas said, worried. "Is the song back?"

"Yeah, but it's different," Shane said. "Louder here than before, and it blends with the sound of the storm."

"You're getting the visions more often."

Shane looked away, then nodded. "Yeah. I didn't say anything because it didn't seem important. And it still might not be. I mean, we've seen some weird shit since everything changed. Maybe my brain is just trying to process it."

"But your 'intuition' has been getting stronger, and I've seen more ghosts," Lucas countered. "I don't think we can just brush it off."

He shifted to see Shane better. "Try to remember the dream. What happened?"

Shane took a deep breath and closed his eyes. "We were on a trail, going into the woods. I didn't recognize where we were, but it looked like a park. And I felt like there was a voice, speaking to me, just beyond the range I could hear what it was saying. That's it. I didn't feel threatened, just that it called to me."

"I was going to suggest going to see the witches in Bedford, to find out if they picked up anything about Raven Rock. I think they'd be the perfect ones to ask about the 'songs' you're hearing," Lucas said.

Shane shrugged uncomfortably. "Maybe. I guess. We'll see. Seems kinda unimportant, with everything else that's going on."

"It's on the way to Gettysburg, and we'll need a place to re-provision," Lucas argued.

"The witches still give me the creeps," Shane admitted.

Lucas raised an eyebrow. "You get visions. I see ghosts. I think we passed creepy a long time ago."

5

By morning, the storm had passed. Worried residents climbed stiffly from their sleeping spots on the floor and ventured out to see what the winds and water had made of their enclave. Kevin was busy from daybreak, directing efforts to clear away the damage and determine how much would require rebuilding.

"We can stay for a while if you need extra hands," Lucas offered.

Kevin shook his head. "Thank you, but you've got more important things to do, and we have plenty of folks to do the work." He sighed, looking out over the wet and windswept "kingdom." "So far, it's just some roofs gone, a couple of older wooden buildings down. Two casualties. It could have been much worse."

"Have you had any other visitors?" Shane asked. "News?"

Kevin nodded. "Had a couple of peddlers through here a week or two ago. What they'd heard from New England isn't good. Early winter blizzards and rising storm surge. Anyone who hadn't pulled inland before doesn't have much choice now."

"We've heard similar about much of the coast," Lucas said.

"So I've been told." Kevin sighed. "I'm also hearing reports of some enclaves going dark. No one's been out to confirm. But we haven't been able to raise them on the shortwave radio, or the emergency telegraph."

"If you know the locations of the enclaves you've lost touch with, we can check in on them if our route takes us that way," Lucas offered.

Kevin rattled off some names, and Lucas jotted them down. "It'll take us a bit with the circuit we ride, but we'll see what we can find out," he promised. "And we'll give these locations to the IT Priests. If there's a college nearby, they can pass the word along and get someone to check."

"Thank you. I'm glad you paid us a visit, even if the storm drove you here," Kevin said. "We do all right; I shouldn't complain, and I'm not, really. But we're cut off these days, like everyone. It's nice to hear that there's a world outside the stockade."

"Not as much of one as there used to be, but plenty of people doing their fucking best to survive," Shane replied.

Kevin nodded gravely. "So say we all."

"It's louder here. Are you sure you can't hear anything?" Shane asked after they'd ridden a short distance from Cooper's Lake.

Lucas shook his head. "I don't hear anything except birds. But does it matter that you keep saying you hear something when we're in a forest or near parkland? Because we're coming up on Moraine."

"Maybe. I don't have any idea," Shane admitted.

Lucas shrugged. "I figured we should stop in to see how

Mitchell was doing, anyhow, since we're riding past. Maybe he'll know something about it."

Shane looked uncomfortable but nodded. "I guess it couldn't hurt."

Moraine State Park's rolling hills had been shaped long ago by glaciers, leaving behind a lake and beautiful scenery. Shane and Lucas rode into what had been the main parking lot. RVs and vehicles parked along the edges, and soggy tents filled the campsites, people who had left everything behind except for what they could pack and ended up here. The park had basic facilities, and a stocked lake, so Lucas guessed there were worse places to sit out the end of the world.

Lucas and Shane tethered their horses and went to the office. Park Ranger Mitchell Wilson greeted them with a surprised smile when he answered the door.

"Lucas and Shane—what an unexpected pleasure. Come on in. I've got a fire going and a hot pot of coffee. You need anything for your horses?"

Lucas shook his head. "They'll be fine. We can't stay long, just wanted to check in—and ask a couple of questions."

"I'm happy for the company. This way," Mitchell said, gesturing for them to follow him into the cozy lobby of the ranger station. Mitchell shared the station as both office and living quarters with another ranger, and they took turns with the outdoor work. "Jim's out checking the trails," he said, referencing his fellow ranger. "We had plenty of limbs down and trail washouts after the storm. We put up as many of the tent folks in the recreation building as we could to ride out the worst of it. There's going to be a lot of work to do to clean up. It's hard to keep up on the maintenance."

"Can't you press some of your squatters…I mean, residents, into working off their use fee?" Shane asked as Mitchell poured coffee for all of them.

"Oh, I do," Mitchell assured him. "But not all of them are

up to the work. We get by," he added with a shrug. "Now, what brings you this way?"

"We've heard that people passing by think there's something different about the park," Shane ventured, fudging a little about his own experience. "Almost a sense that calls to them. Have you heard anything like that?"

Mitchell sat back, cradling his coffee. "Now that's interesting," he replied. "Truth is, those of us who chose to work the parks always felt a bit of that. Where we've felt it the strongest, we applied to be posted. Haven't you ever heard people say that a location 'spoke' to them?"

"I guess so," Lucas agreed reluctantly. "But I didn't mean it literally."

Mitchell nodded. "You might not have, but many cultures think that there are nature spirits. Maybe there's something to all that, and the shake-up from the Events means the spirits can be heard again.

"All I can tell you is that I loved Moraine from the first time I laid eyes on it, like I found somewhere I should have always been. Jim said he felt the same way. So, was it just a combination of all the features we always wanted or did the park 'claim' us? I don't know. I'm just glad to be here, even with all the shit going on outside."

They spent another hour catching Mitchell up on what they had seen and passing along a warning about the prepper activities. Mitchell filled them in on what the refugees who had taken up residence in the park told him about the places they came from. Some of the information was true, but Shane and Lucas knew much of it was hearsay, exaggerated, or just plain wrong.

"We need to get going," Lucas said after they had finished their coffee. "Still have to get to Bedford."

"Glad you stopped in," Mitchell replied, setting his cup aside. "Do me a favor, and if you see any peddlers on the road, send them this way. We do all right for food, but things like pots and pans, knives, and that sort of thing are in short supply."

"Will do," Shane promised, and they headed back to their mounts.

"So?" Lucas asked as they swung up to their saddles. "Did the park say anything to you?"

Shane rolled his eyes. "Fuck you."

"That's a strange thing for the park to say," Lucas replied. "Since it doesn't even know me."

"Maybe it's all-seeing," Shane said as they headed back to the road. "And it already knows how annoying you can be."

"Is that a no?" Lucas pressed.

"I'm not sure," Shane answered. "It's hard to put into words. The whole time we were talking with Mitchell, I could swear I heard faint singing, just at the edge of what I could make out."

"Do you think there's something to what he said, about places having a spirit?"

"Lots of cultures believe that," Shane said.

"When we get to Old Bedford, I bet the witches will know," Lucas replied. "Folks like them have to know something about nature spirits."

"If they don't, the scholars will," Shane said. "You know, with all the shit that's happened, one of the good things is seeing the historic villages come back to life."

"Don't forget we're heading to Gettysburg," Lucas warned. "That's one location I really could do without seeing come back to how it used to be."

Living history museums, like Old Bedford Village, had been uniquely ready to weather the end of modern civilization. Since the sites were dedicated to preserving and teaching the old ways of living, the volunteers and staff had the skills necessary to survive when the outside world collapsed. The Old Bedford folks moved into the historic homes and brought the museum back to life as a real village, working the land, raising animals, and using what they'd learned about old skills like weaving and forging iron. Already a magnet for history buffs, the old sites also tended to attract covens and academics that needed a new home.

Did those sites also have a spirit, and did it call to the witches and scholars? Lucas wondered. Now that Shane and Mitchell had raised the question, Lucas found he couldn't stop thinking about it.

They fell into their usual companionable silence as they road. The highway was empty aside from themselves, making it seem all the more desolate, an eight-lane throughway with no traffic. Just in case, they had weapons handy. Lucas kept his crossbow slung over his shoulder and his quarrels within reach, while Shane had a large machete in a sheath on his belt and a selection of throwing knives in a bandolier slung across his chest. Their shotguns were handy, and the rest of their weapons and ammunition were in the saddlebags. In the dead stretches between settlements, they'd learned the hard way that anything could be lurking—human, animal, or something much worse.

Lucas was just happy that the rain held off. It would take more than three days to reach Old Bedford, and Lucas really didn't want to be hunkered down against bad weather for the whole time. They spent the first night in an abandoned house, and the second in a sturdy barn, and as evening loomed on the third night, Lucas found himself hoping to find a place that was both dry and warm.

"You know what we were saying about places having a vibe to them?" Shane asked. "If that's true, then I don't like what I'm sensing from this hollow. Let's pick up the pace. It feels...wrong."

Lucas had looked over to Shane as he spoke. When he

turned his attention back to the road, he saw a young girl standing in the middle of the highway.

"Whoa!" He pulled in on the reins sharply, and Shane did the same.

"What?" Shane asked. "What's the problem?"

Lucas pointed at the girl. "Don't you see her?" The girl waved her arms, and while she remained silent, the message of warning was clear.

"There's no one there, Lucas," Shane replied. "I think it's one of your sightings. All the more reason for us to get gone."

The ghost girl vanished as Shane spoke, proving his point.

"Then I second your heebie-jeebies and vote we find a place to hole up, pronto."

"Heads up!" Shane warned, as the pounding of hoof beats sounded just over the rise ahead.

Four men on horseback crested the hill, riding abreast. Three of them carried swords, and the fourth had a rifle. They stopped, blocking the highway.

"Stop right there," the leader said. "We don't want trouble. Just leave us your saddlebags and your horses, and we'll let you walk away, no hard feelings."

6

"Fuck you," Lucas replied. "Not going to happen."

The man with the rifle brought it up to his shoulder. "You might want to reconsider."

Shane's throwing knife embedded itself deep in the rifleman's bicep, and the thief screamed, dropping the weapon. The other three robbers rode forward, swords raised. Lucas leveled his crossbow and fired, and the bolt hit the lead rider hard enough to unseat him. The man fell, dead before he hit the ground.

The remaining thieves barely slowed their pace, riding toward Lucas and Shane with a war whoop. Lucas loaded another crossbow bolt and held his position, confident his bolt could reach its mark long before the brigand's sword was in range. Shane pulled a shotgun from its sheath on his saddle and aimed for the man in front, blasting him with a spray of buckshot, sending him toppling from his horse. Lucas's second bolt took the third man through the right shoulder, leaving him alive but wounded.

That left two dead thieves, and two bleeding. Shane

racked his gun again, looking down the barrel at the two survivors. "Don't try my patience."

The youngest of the thieves reined in his horse, raising his hands in surrender. "Don't shoot me. I told them this was a bad idea."

"Yeah?" Lucas replied. "And that was before you tried to rob two US Marshals."

The two men paled at that.

"Shit," the younger thief said. He had the crossbow bolt in his shoulder. "I said this was going to be trouble," he griped, turning to the companion with Shane's knife in his arm. "Didn't I? And you thought it would be easy pickings."

"Shut up, Danny."

"This is all your fault!" Danny shouted. "Next time, you'd better goddamn listen when I tell you something won't work!"

Shane glanced at Lucas and rolled his eyes. "All right," Shane ordered. "Get down off your horses, and keep your hands where we can see them. Lie down on the ground, with your hands behind your heads."

"He's gonna shoot us," Danny whined. "Gonna shoot us dead, and you said this was going to be easy!"

"Shut the fuck up, Danny!"

Lucas held his crossbow on the men while Shane kept his shotgun at the ready as he moved among the brigands, kicking their weapons away from them.

"Danny, I'm going to give you some rope, and you're going to tie your buddy nice and tight," Lucas said. "I'll check the knots, so if you try something, I'll know, and you'll be sorry." He pulled several lengths of rope from his saddle bag and tossed them to Danny, not getting close enough for the thief to make a grab for his bow.

"This one's dead," Shane reported, from where he bent over the man with the crossbow bolt in his chest. He paused next to the man he'd gotten with the shotgun. "So is he."

He turned his attention to the two wounded survivors, glancing first at the man with the knife in his bicep. "We need to tie up his wound." He looked at Danny. "Rip a strip of cloth from your shirt and bind his arm up. Don't want him bleeding out on the ride. Once he's tied up, we'll see to your injury."

"Derek and Tom are dead, Ben!" Danny shrilled. "And we're gonna bleed out. All because of you and your fucking bright idea."

"I'm gonna kill you if you don't shut up," Ben, the man with the knife wound, grated.

Danny was so nervous he dropped the rope several times, but he managed to get the knots right, finally. Shane bound up Danny's wound around the quarrel and then tied him up while Lucas covered them. "I'm leaving the arrow in until you get where you're going, to help seal the wound. It's a hunting tip, so it should be easy to take out."

"Are you gonna hang us?" Danny asked, and his voice cracked with the fear.

"We could," Lucas replied, looking as if he was thinking it over. "What do you think?" he asked Shane.

"Not worth the rope," Shane replied, gathering up the weapons. "Although we'd be within our rights."

"You ever heard of the US Marshals?" Lucas asked. Danny shook his head, still face down on the ground. Ben grunted, so scared that he'd pissed himself. "Since the Events, we're the law in our territory. So we can be judge, jury, and executioner."

"I don't wanna die!" Danny wailed. "We haven't done much thieving, I promise. We're new at it, that's why we suck."

"Shut your mouth!" Ben snarled.

"Well, your horses are pretty much crap," Shane said. "Where did you get the swords?"

"My dad used to make them, for Renaissance festivals and conventions," Ben replied grudgingly. "Had them lying all around the house."

"That explains why none of them have a real edge on them." Shane gathered up the swords and leaned down for the rifle. "Aw, fuck. Seriously? It wasn't loaded."

"We figured it would scare you into giving us all your shit," Danny said. He rolled close enough to Ben to give him a swift kick with his bound feet. Ben tried to retaliate but went still and quiet when Shane stuck the tip of a sword against his neck.

"This may not be sharp, but sawing away at you until your head falls off wouldn't be pleasant," Shane promised. "Get my drift?"

"What're you gonna do with us?" Danny asked, and the quaver in his voice made Shane re-evaluate the man's age, guessing him to be in his late teens.

"We're gonna dump you and your crap horses at the next enclave for the sheriff to deal with," Lucas said. "The dead guys, we leave for the vultures, as a warning to the next sons of bitches who decided to loot travelers. We take your weapons, so you aren't tempted to do something like this again—assuming the sheriff doesn't just throw you down a mine shaft and let you rot."

Danny squeaked, looking pale enough to pass out. Ben muttered curses that trailed off into a moan.

Shane patted them down, taking away anything else that could be used as a weapon. Then he and Lucas hoisted the wannabe highwaymen onto their horses, belly down across the saddle, and tied the reins of the dead men's horses to the last saddle. Lucas rode point, and Shane road behind, making sure neither of the thieves tried to escape.

The sheriff at the next enclave looked none too happy to see them. "What do you want me to do with them?"

"Anything you want," Lucas said. "Thought they might be local, and you'd want to take that into consideration. My partner and I have places to be. Didn't have time to hang them."

"Yeah, they're local," the sheriff replied. "Not the first time they've been in trouble, but they're usually too dumb to pull it off." He glared at the bound men. "I'm thinking I'll put them on work detail, get some use out of them, instead of throwing them a necktie party. We've got some digging and shoveling that suits them just fine. Might be the first honest work they've ever done."

"They're all yours," Shane said, as he and Lucas headed back to the road. He had tied the swords behind his saddle and meant to see if he could give them a working edge with a good whetstone when time permitted. He and Lucas rode in silence until they were back on the road.

"You didn't actually want to hang them." Shane's tone made it a statement, not a question.

"Not particularly," Lucas replied, looking off toward the horizon. "Seen enough death, don't need to see more."

"But the preppers—"

"That was different." Lucas's voice turned hard. "They weren't just going to take someone's coins. They killed. They enjoyed killing. How long until they weren't happy to just wait for travelers to come to them and started raiding the other enclaves?"

"I didn't mind scaring the shit out of this last bunch, but I really didn't want to go through with hanging them, either," Shane agreed.

"As it is, two of them're dead anyhow." Lucas's voice was flat, and Shane knew that meant the death bothered his partner. "And the guy with the shoulder wound is gonna lose that arm, if he survives."

"Not your fault," Shane replied.

"I shot him. He attacked with a weapon," Lucas said, but it sounded like he was trying to convince himself. They would have been entirely within their mandate to have killed all four of the men, since highway robbery and horse theft had regained their status as capital offenses. Still, Shane felt unsettled over the man's death, and he could tell Lucas did, too.

"I hate when it goes like that."

They rode for a while, and Lucas seemed pensive. Finally, Shane decided to poke the bear. "What's eating you? You're not usually this quiet. I mean, half the time I can't get you to shut up."

Lucas shrugged. "Not sure how I feel about the ghost thing, I guess."

"Oh, so it's okay when I have visions, but you see a ghost, and it's the end of the world?"

Lucas gave him a look. "We've already had the end of the world, dumbass." He paused. "It's just not something I ever really took seriously, you know? I heard about it from my mom and grandma, and I had some experiences I couldn't really explain away, so I just didn't think about them."

"But now, it's happening more often, in ways you can't just write off," Shane supplied.

"Yeah. Just like your 'hunches' and 'intuition' and 'gut feelings' are turning into full crystal-ball-reading style visions."

Shane grimaced. "I have never, ever, used a crystal ball. Wouldn't know what to do with one if I had it—maybe throw it at someone?" He gave Lucas a side glance. "I mean, now that you're a ghost whisperer, are you going to start knocking on tables and talking in funny voices?"

"Shut up," Lucas said, but there was no heat in his voice. Shane grinned. They'd argued far more heatedly over which superheroes could beat each other up. If the world had to fall apart, it was nice to still have his best friend.

They spent the night holed up at what used to be a Motel 6. Shane suspected that the only reason it hadn't been filled by squatters was that half the roof had been torn off. The office had been flattened by a long-ago storm. He and Lucas found a room at the end of the row and considered themselves lucky since they'd slept in much worse accommodations. The carpet wasn't quite as disgusting as Shane expected, which he attributed to the room's windows remaining intact.

Shane's dreams were restless. He heard a new voice and a different song. In the darkness of his dream, Shane couldn't see the body that went with the voice, but he felt the same odd presence he had sensed before.

Hello? he called into the void. *I hear you singing. What are you? And where are you? Why can I hear you?*

The voice kept on singing, but Shane had the feeling the entity behind it had drawn closer, studying him. He didn't feel afraid, just overwhelmingly curious. An image came to mind, of him riding his horse, seen from a distance. More images followed the first. No words, just images, and a song.

Yes, that's me. Can you show me what you look like?

The song continued, but Shane could have sworn it sounded pensive, maybe even melancholy.

Are you the song? You're not showing me what you look like because I can't see you?

The song picked up tempo, sounding more cheerful.

Are you the being from Moraine? Once again, the music slowed. *You're from somewhere close to here?* An upbeat tempo was his answer.

Why contact me if I can't see you?

The music took on a wistful note. Shane felt an overwhelming loneliness sweep over him, choking him up. *You're lonely?* Again, the music shifted to a happier tempo. *And I can sense you, is that it? Most people can't, or they don't sense you strongly enough to communicate?* The music stayed happy.

Thank you, Shane said, as the dream began to waver. He woke in the same position he'd fallen asleep, huddled against the wall. Moonlight streamed in through the deteriorating curtains, giving enough of a glow to see the room around him.

"Bad dream?" Lucas sat in a chair on watch, and of course he'd noticed Shane twitching in his sleep.

Shane shifted, aware that his leg had fallen asleep. If it wasn't time for his watch, he might as well get up anyhow, since he wouldn't be dozing again tonight. "Vision. There's another…entity…nearby. Like at Moraine, and the other places. It didn't talk to me, but it showed me pictures, and it changed its song to answer my questions."

"It responded to you?" Lucas looked up sharply. Shane nodded.

"Yeah. And not just yes/no answers. It gave me the impression it was lonely." He met Lucas's gaze. "Whatever these entities are, I think they're sentient, and they can understand emotions."

"That's a bit of a stretch, isn't it?"

"Not from what I just saw," Shane replied. "Now I really want to know what the witches have to say. Because there was also that weird feeling I got when the ghost girl showed up on the road, that we were in a bad place. So whatever these energies are, we need to know how to deal with the ones that aren't friendly."

Lucas shifted in the uncomfortable plastic chair. "You think they're dangerous?"

"I don't think they have to be. The one in Moraine didn't

seem to be trying to hurt anyone, and neither did the one in my vision. But if they can be strong in good places, maybe they can be just as strong in bad places, and that could be a problem."

"Then let's hope the witches know what the hell is going on," Lucas said, getting up to change places with Shane so he could get some sleep. "Because I sure as fuck don't want to find out the hard way."

7

They reached Bedford just after lunch. Before they headed for the restored historic village, Shane convinced Lucas to let him try to sense the presence he had communicated with in his dreams.

"What is this, some kind of supernatural game of Marco Polo?" Lucas asked after they had ridden almost to the other side of town.

"You're not wrong," Shane replied, pulling out of his thoughts. "But I think we're close."

"Wouldn't it be likely to be in a park, or maybe at the restored village?"

Shane shrugged. "I don't know how they pick their places. Maybe those weren't 'sacred' enough."

Lucas's expression was skeptical, but he said nothing as Shane continued to follow a vague gut feeling that he was going in the right direction. He let the horse watch the road for obstacles, making a few course corrections as they went, focused on the song only he could hear. As it grew stronger, Shane felt certain they were headed in the right direction. Finally, when the song grew loud and he sensed the brush of a familiar presence against his mind, he stopped.

"Here?" Lucas asked, sounding genuinely surprised.

Shane pulled himself out of his thoughts and found that he was staring at a giant, silver-painted, three-story building at the edge of a fairgrounds. The building looked like a coffee pot. "Um, I guess so?"

"I've never seen a sacred coffee pot before."

Shane consulted his inner sense, thinking he must have made a mistake, only to hear the song more strongly than ever. The song was loud near the roadside attraction, but even louder directly across the road.

"I remember reading somewhere that the same thing that makes one person build a temple might make another build an amusement park," Shane mused. "They're both places where people transcend their usual, everyday lives."

Lucas laughed. "You mean I could have been on a roller coaster instead of going to Mass? Man, did I get the short end of the stick!"

Shane felt a little chagrined, but he knew he was correct. "Think about it. Some places are supposed to be healthy or lucky, and some get the reputation for having 'bad vibes.' People travel hundreds of miles to go to tourist attractions that make them feel happy, or to see 'natural wonders' that give them a feeling of peace."

"Well, they used to," Lucas replied. "Not so much anymore."

"You know what I mean."

Lucas nudged his horse to ride up beside Shane. "Yeah, yeah. I think I do. And maybe it's not that far-fetched. But dude, a giant coffee pot?"

Shane grinned. "Could have been a giant ball of string. Or a huge cowboy boot. Or a big hollow elephant." He had no idea how those famous attractions had fared after the Events, but part of him hoped they were still standing, a tribute to human whimsy in a world that desperately needed it.

They headed back to the historic village, both deep in thought. The entity Shane had sensed did not try to reach out to him again.

Old Bedford Village had been a historic collection of preserved and restored buildings before the Cataclysm gave it a new life. As a tourist attraction, reenactors dressed in period clothing demonstrated spinning, weaving, and candle making. After the Events, those skills and others like them were in high demand. It hadn't taken much for the docents to move in and put their skills to use. Professors and students from nearby colleges sought refuge, as did townsfolk and a local coven, creating an eclectic mix.

The Pendergrass Tavern was the social heart of the village. The handsome building had a first floor of stacked stone and a log-and-mortar second floor. When the museum had catered to tourists, the tavern had been a working restaurant. Now, it still served as a pub and gathering place.

Lucas led the way. At this hour, just before dusk, the pub was fairly quiet. Shane felt sure it would get busier once full dark fell and people ended their chores. Candles in glass hurricane shades lit each table, and a fire in the fireplace at the end of the common room cast a welcoming glow.

"Two of your ales, and two plowman's meals," Lucas ordered. The bartender returned with two pint glasses of dark, pub-brewed ale, and two wooden boards laden with bread, cheese, sliced ham, pickles, onions, and hard-boiled eggs.

"What brings you two back to Bedford?" Jake, the proprietor of the Pendergrass, asked as he took their money and made change. "Something happen to bring the Marshals our way?"

"Something's always happening, nowadays," Shane

replied. "Can you put us up for the night? We got in just before the rain."

"Sure," Jake replied. "Same room you had the last time, twin beds and a washstand. Just remodeled the outhouse behind the pub. Not exactly luxury, but you won't get splinters in your ass."

"Always a good thing," Lucas replied. "How's it going?"

Jake shrugged. "We've had some bad storms through, but I guess that's probably true everywhere. We've gotten good at battening the hatches and hunkering down. This one didn't do as much damage as some, so there's that."

"Your ale is getting better," Shane said, sipping his drink.

Jake grinned. "Good to hear you say so. We've been tinkering with the recipe." Before the Events, Jake had been a chemistry professor and a part-time docent. Now, he put his background to good use with the enclave's brewing, distilling, and winery.

"Generator still working?" Lucas asked.

"Mostly," Jake replied, and paused to pour another round for two customers farther down the bar. "It's pretty much only running the big refrigerator/freezer in the back and the power for the medical center Doc Forrest put in over in the Victorian House," he added. "Pete keeps the generator going on spit and salvaged parts. Of course, it helped that we cleaned out Home Depot after everyone else died off or left town."

"Have you seen Scott Findlay?" Shane asked. "We need to talk to him. Karen Becker, too, if she's around."

Jake raised an eyebrow. "Two US Marshals walk into a bar. They ask to see the boss man and the head witch. Sounds like the start of a bad joke…or a big problem."

"Hopefully, neither," Lucas replied. "Just looking for information right now."

"They're not here," Jake said. "But I can send my busboy, Jimmy, to go fetch them."

"I'd be much obliged." Lucas leaned against the bar and began to pick at the food, and Jake went in the back to send Jimmy on his way.

Shane looked around the pub as Lucas and Jake talked. The patrons looked like something out of a time-travel movie, with some who had worked at the museum preferring to keep their period garb, while others stuck to modern clothing. Shane wondered what their occupations had been prior to the Cataclysm, and what they found themselves doing now.

"You two can go on into the back room with your food, and I'll send Scott and Karen in when they get here," Jake said. They picked up their things to go. "Oh, before I forget," Jake added, "we have a couple of IT Priests who came in last night, asked if we'd seen you. Said they had a message."

Shane and Lucas exchanged a look. "Guess we know where we're headed after this," Lucas said. They thanked Jake and took their food to a small room off the main area, where they settled in at a hand-hewn wooden table.

"Want to bet this has something to do with the IOT breakdown?" Shane asked once they polished off most of their meal.

"Yeah, that's what I think, too," Lucas agreed. "Considering that the universities still have internet? I'm betting Gibbons up at Slippery Rock probably told Tony Brown over at Shippensburg that we were heading this way, and Tony found something out that was important enough to have the priests looking for us."

"I can't say I'm looking forward to Gettysburg," Lucas said, finishing off his last pickle. "Not with the sightings happening more and more."

"Shit," Shane replied. "I hadn't thought about that."

Gettysburg was one of the most haunted places in America. Lucas's growing talent for seeing ghosts could make their visit very unpleasant.

"Maybe I can wear some garlic, keep them at bay."

"That's for vampires, not ghosts."

"Didn't do squat with the last vamps we ran into," Lucas replied. "Maybe ghosts are more sensitive to bad breath."

Before Shane could reply, they heard footsteps approaching. Shane looked up and saw Scott Findlay and Karen Becker come into the back room, both looking either worried or annoyed.

"Marshals," Findlay said with a nod, greeting them both with a handshake. Findlay had been the museum director Before and became the mayor of the enclave when the museum village came back to life as a working community. He *looked* like a museum director, Shane thought, with a slight pot belly, a trimmed white beard, and a penchant for mixing period garb and modern pieces that made him look like he'd raided a closet on the TARDIS.

"Shane and Lucas. This is unexpected." Karen Becker resembled a suburban soccer mom more than a powerful witch and head of the local coven. Her dark brown hair was trimmed in a neat bob cut, proving that even the apocalypse couldn't separate some people from their grooming routines, and she wore an Aran wool sweater over jeans and hiking boots under a sensible parka.

Findlay and Karen took seats at the table, and Jake showed up a few minutes later with a fresh round of pints for everyone. Findlay cleared his throat.

"So, what's going on? You weren't just in the neighborhood."

"We're heading south of Gettysburg, where apparently, a big enclave went dark," Lucas said. "But most of all, we wanted to pick your brains about the…entities…that seem to be present in some of the state parks."

"Entities?" Karen asked, leaning forward. "You mean, like ghosts?"

Shane shook his head. "More like an invisible, sentient, empathic presence that sings," he said. *What if she just tells me I'm crazy?*

"Sounds like a genius loci," Findlay said, and Karen nodded. "You've sensed this…entity yourselves?"

"Just me," Shane confessed. "I've been having dreams for a while, on and off, where I heard strange singing. When we went to one of the state parks, I recognized the kind of song, and I've heard it since then—including at the big coffee pot here in Bedford."

Shane braced himself for their laughter. Instead, both Karen and Findlay looked at him like he had suddenly become fascinating.

"You said it was sentient and empathic," Karen pressed. "How do you know?"

Shane recounted his dreams and the encounters with the "songs." As he spoke, Karen worried at her lower lip, deep in thought. She exchanged another glance with Findlay. "It's definitely a genius loci. The nature spirits are waking up."

"What, exactly, is a genius loci?" Lucas asked. "Is it really smart?"

Findlay chuckled. "It's sentient, which is the old meaning to the word. 'Guardian spirit' is probably a better translation, or 'spirit of a place.'" He sounded like he was gearing up for a lecture until Karen laid a hand on his arm.

"It's a type of daemon," Karen continued. "Very old. They were here before we evolved, and they'll be here after we're gone."

"You said these spirits were waking up," Shane asked. "Why did they go to sleep? And why wake up now?"

"The daemons never went away, but the noise and bustle of modern civilization didn't seem to suit them," Karen replied. "Some of them hung on at places like the Grand Canyon, or the biggest tourist attractions. The rest just went to sleep, until their time came again."

"So are they good or bad?" Shane pressed. "Because I've had both impressions, depending on where I was."

"I'm not sure that's exactly the right question to ask," Findlay replied. "Because for an ancient, primal being, our ideas of good and bad are a little simplistic. Think of them more as being in alignment with chaos or creation. So the daemons that people consider to be healing, peaceful, and restorative would be attuned to creation energy. And the ones that have attached themselves to places that make people uneasy or frightened are aligned with chaos."

"But I definitely picked up on emotions," Shane insisted. "The song changed its tempo and whether it was in a major or minor key to answer my questions. It definitely seemed to be empathic."

"Interesting," Karen mused. "Maybe they're reverting to a more primal version of themselves since the Events."

"Or perhaps, with all the forces at work in the world right now, even the daemons are changing," Findlay speculated. "After all, your people have reported shifts in their abilities."

Karen nodded. "Since the Events, even very seasoned witches are discovering that their powers don't work the way they did Before."

"Think of all the big forces at play," Findlay said, after taking a drink of his ale. "A huge outburst of radiation when the bombs hit the world's major capitals. And then the aftermath of the explosions. Volcanic eruptions and tsunamis—both of which, by the way, were once believed to be entities in their own right. Powerful hurricanes and earthquakes. Climate shifts. Reactor meltdowns. And that tectonic fissure out west that turned the Yellowstone Caldera into Centralia on steroids. That's fucking with the bones of the world," he said, his eyes alight with a scholar's glee. "Why wouldn't that kind of disruption affect the most primal energies of all?"

Shane sat back, trying to process what they'd said. *I didn't imagine it. I'm not crazy. And what the hell does it mean that I can hear daemons and communicate with them?*

"So are these daemons friend or foe?" Lucas asked.

Karen shrugged. "They do what they do for their own reasons, and if that helps or hinders an individual, it's not intentional."

"Great," Lucas replied, setting his empty pint glass down a little harder than necessary. "We don't just have to worry about everything else—now we've got demons on the loose."

"Daemons," Karen corrected. "Completely different. Demons are infernal. Daemons are natural spirits."

Shane opened his mouth to ask about demons, and shut it again without saying anything. He was still wrapping his mind around ghosts, shifters, and monsters being real. He wasn't ready to think about demons, too.

"So, why are these daemons stalking Shane?" Lucas asked. Shane had to smile at the protective tone, something that had always been there since they were kids. Lucas trounced bullies on the playground. Shane beat the pants off them in the classroom.

"I don't think they're 'stalking' him any more than the ghosts are 'stalking' you," Karen replied. "Did you know that we've been getting one or two people every month or so coming to find the coven because they've suddenly found themselves with psychic gifts they never knew they had before and don't know what to do?"

She looked from Lucas to Shane. "In the first year after the Events, it was just a few. More the next year, and now almost a steady stream. What happened to the world changed everything. It changed *us*."

"Think of it as upgrading your subscription and being able to stream new channels. The daemons and ghosts were always there, but you weren't receiving a clear signal. Now, there's less interference," Findlay said.

"Shit," Lucas said. "They definitely didn't cover that in Basic Training."

"I'll get a couple of my coven sisters to come over and start your training. You won't learn it all in one sitting, but you'll at least have some basics to practice that can help you gain control and shield yourselves," Karen offered.

"When do you want to start?" Shane asked, and gave Lucas a kick under the table.

"I'm in," Lucas added, in a voice that was less than enthusiastic.

"Give me two hours to put out the word, and we'll meet you here," Karen replied.

8

"You want me to sit still while you attack me?" Lucas's eyebrows practically crawled up his forehead. They had settled in a quiet room with a cozy fire and comfortable pillows for sitting on the floor. Shane felt intrigued at the opportunity to learn from the witches, but he wasn't surprised that Lucas's reaction was far more skeptical.

Karen shook her head. "Not a physical attack. A psychic one."

Lucas quirked a thumb at Shane. "He's the one with mojo. I just shoot things."

Karen shot a look at Shane for support. He just smiled and nodded, confirming what she already had probably figured out about Lucas. Shane loved him like a brother, but Lucas could be a serious asshole when he wanted to be.

"And if you don't learn to shield as much as possible, then you become a liability, a distraction, a target which will get your partner dead," Karen replied evenly, narrowing her eyes in challenge.

Shane bit back a snort, wishing he had popcorn to watch

the battle of wills. Karen had nailed Lucas's soft spot, and from the grim line of his partner's mouth, Lucas knew it.

"Fine. But don't blame me if it's a waste of time," Lucas muttered.

Lucas and Shane settled in, crossing their legs and getting comfortable. Even when he closed his eyes, Shane could sense Lucas's impatience. He didn't need to look at this friend to know Lucas was twitching—jiggling his knee, tapping his fingers, biting his lip. Lucas never sat completely still, unless he was on sniper duty. Then all of that nervous energy turned into lethal focus.

Shane didn't recognize the assault for what it was at first. It started slow and gentle, easily mistaken for meandering thoughts until pulling back turned difficult. He forced himself to take a deep breath and stop struggling, then gathered his resources and pushed back with an effort of will. The invasive thoughts winked out.

Beside him, Lucas's restlessness took on a more frantic cast, and he swore under his breath. Shane opened his eyes and saw his friend's face twist in discomfort, while Lucas's entire body had gone rigid with the effort of fighting off the mental incursion.

All of a sudden, Lucas fell forward, released from the assault. The glower on his face told Shane that the other man knew he'd been let go, instead of freeing himself.

"Now you see what I mean," Karen said mildly. Lucas glared but wisely kept his thoughts to himself.

"So we can use these skills to keep from being distracted by entities like the daemons?" Shane asked.

Karen nodded. "Distraction would be the least invasive, but it could be deadly if it disrupted your focus in the middle of a fight."

"What kind of attack do you really think is likely?" Lucas wiped the sweat from his forehead. Despite his skeptical attitude, he looked flushed from the effort of fighting off the mental assault. That meant he was taking the training seriously, Shane knew.

"This."

Between one breath and the next, Shane found himself plunged back into the chaos of the first weeks after the Events.

Shane felt panic rise as he dialed every number in his contact list, to no avail. Even their emergency numbers got no answer. Some of those official numbers were supposed to be valid in the event of an attack, but planning had obviously fallen short of reality.

Worse, Shane got no answer when he tried to reach his family.

"Maybe the towers are down," he'd said. Lucas looked up from his own phone, and the desolation on his face said everything Shane needed to know.

"Hey, fellas," Vinnie Scarpelli said, pointing toward the TV on the wall with a sick look on his face.

Only one TV channel still worked, and it ran a no-frills, one-camera news marathon reporting whatever information the crew could gather. Since the internet was as spotty as the cell phones, news beyond the local area was nearly impossible to come by, and what Shane had seen merely confirmed they were all fucked.

"We have confirmation that Washington, D.C. and several other major capital cities around the world were hit with nearly simultaneous nuclear strikes," the haggard anchor reported. Without makeup or hairstyling, he looked as if someone had grabbed him off the street and stuck him in front of the camera. Pale and wide-eyed, he had ended up as the voice of the Cataclysm.

"Did you hear that?" Vinnie screeched. "Bombs. Lots of them. Oh god, this is bad. This is real bad."

Shane stared at his useless phone as the call to his dad's number rang without an answer...

No! I lived this once. Not again. Shane mustered his will and slowed his breathing, taking a mental step back from the horror the vision forced him to relive. This time, instead of pushing back, he envisioned high, impervious castle walls made of thick stone. He built the wall piece by piece, until nothing remained of Vinnie, the frightened news anchor, or the memory of the day everything ended.

Inside his mental fortress, Shane breathed a sigh of relief. The quiet was a balm, shutting out the noise and the loss. But gradually, Shane became aware that he was rocking back and forth, as the motion grew harder to ignore.

His control snapped, the walls fell, and he realized that someone's fingers dug painfully into his upper arm, jerking him from one side to the other.

"Hey! Wake up!" Lucas yelled. Shane's eyes opened, and he saw his partner's worried face only inches from his own. "You got lost inside your head," Lucas explained, letting go and sitting back. "I was afraid I'd get lost in all the empty space if they made me go in after you," he added with a lopsided smirk that didn't hide the worry in his eyes.

"You did a little too well," Karen said, eying Shane as if he were a puzzle. "Excellent shielding for someone without training, but if you aren't careful, you could wall yourself away so well you can't respond to a physical threat."

"Or give your partner a heart attack," Lucas muttered. "I wasn't sure you could find your way home."

Shane could see that despite his bluster, Lucas had been rattled by whatever vision Karen had plunged him into. His gaze was haunted and his jaw clenched. There had been many horrors for the witch to choose from, some worse than others, but all of them bad.

"Have I convinced you that the need is real?" Karen asked,

directing her attention to Lucas, who nodded at the same time he gave a sullen shrug. "Good. Then I'll stop with the demonstrations and get down to work on showing you how to defend yourselves."

Shane and Lucas spent the next two days with the witches, who did their best to pack as much training as possible into a short period of time. Karen also brought protective amulets for both Shane and Lucas, to help safeguard them from gaining the wrong kind of attention. By the end of the marathon session, both men were exhausted, but Shane felt more confident about their ability to defend themselves from a psychic assault.

"Thank you," Shane said as the witches rose to leave. "This is all very new to us. We really appreciate it."

Karen smiled. "Given what you two do, I think on the whole, your new abilities will be more helpful than not. Just remember what we taught you and come back for another lesson when you pass this way again."

Shane had felt certain that he was tired enough to sleep like a rock. But despite how exhausted he felt, his dreams were dark.

Shane looked around, and realized where he was, and when. Youngstown. A year after the bombs hit Washington.

The year the epidemics started.

Bloated, discolored corpses lay stacked like cordwood along city streets, with nowhere to bury them, and no one to come take them away. Flies, rats, and vultures feasted, and spread disease. A new, potent strain of influenza didn't just hit children and the elderly; it seemed to strike hardest at those in their prime. Whole families died, sometimes within a single day. Those who weren't infected fled to save their lives, carrying contagion.

The power grid wasn't dependable, which hit the pumping stations, sewer treatment plants, and reservoir filtering equipment. Gasoline became too scarce to run garbage trucks, so trash piled up in the streets, next to the bodies. Modern cities weren't designed to function without sanitation. Those who didn't die from influenza sickened from typhus or cholera.

Whole sections of Youngstown fell silent, filled with the dead. The decision to do a controlled burn, block by block, made sense. It just didn't work the way anyone planned, not when a sudden storm swept in from the plains, carrying embers aloft and setting half the city on fire.

Shane found himself trapped by the fire. He had gotten separated from Lucas and the others, and now nothing but flames surrounded him. The blaze turned Youngstown's streets into pyres, stinking of burning refuse and charred flesh. Shane gagged, and his eyes watered from the heavy smoke. The flames hadn't reached his section of the street, but it wouldn't be long; he could feel the heat on his skin, stealing his breath.

Lucas, where was Lucas? Shane thought his partner was right behind him, but when he turned back, he found himself alone.

Shane heard the crackle of flames and distant crashes as the fire brought down buildings. An explosion rocked the street and sent bricks tumbling from a nearby facade. Cars, left behind by the dead, became bombs as the fire reached them.

Nowhere to run, no one coming to save him. Shane knew he was going to die.

The song called to him, and he wondered how he could hear it above the din. It touched his mind like cool water, beckoning him to follow. A narrow passageway opened between two tall buildings that were, as yet, untouched by the conflagration. The song grew louder, and with nothing to lose, Shane ventured after it.

No words, just a melody he would never be able to remember enough to hum, and an unspoken promise of safety. Shane ran, covering his mouth and nose with his shirt as ash swirled around him. He didn't know where the corridor led, but if he was going to die, he'd rather do it trying to escape than waiting to be burned alive.

Then he heard it, the rush of water, and he emerged into the blessed rain of pumper trucks doing their best to hold back an inferno. His skin was red and scorched, falling embers burned his hair, and his lungs ached from the smoke, but he was alive, and as the water soaked him, he started to laugh in sheer, delirious relief.

Shane came awake with a start. Lucas stirred from where he sat near the window, his back to the wall so he could watch the door.

"What's wrong?"

Shane raised a trembling hand to wipe his sweat-soaked hair from his face. "I was back in Youngstown. In the fire."

"Shit." Lucas gave him a look. "Was it just a dream? Or was someone trying to get to you?"

"Pretty sure it was just a nightmare—or a memory," Shane replied. "It didn't feel like a vision. But in the dream, I followed a daemon's song to find the path out of the fire. I don't remember that…but, it's possible? I was cut off, I didn't know that part of the city, and I thought I was going to die."

His voice sounded wrecked. "Something made me run the opposite direction I meant to go, and that's when I saw the alley." Shane looked up at Lucas's worried face. "Could it have been a daemon guiding me, even then?"

Lucas pulled a flask from the pocket of his coat and handed it to Shane. "That time in Iraq, when we got turned around in Mosul, and I 'figured out' where to go?" He shook his head. "It wasn't me. There was a ghost, a young boy, who led us out. I didn't say anything because..."

"Yeah."

This time, Lucas met Shane's gaze. "So...what do we do now?"

Shane closed his eyes and let his head fall back against the wall. "We use what the witches taught us. God knows we need every advantage we can get."

9

"Did you just refer to artificial intelligence units as... feral?" Lucas looked at the IT Priest as if he had lost his mind.

"How does that even happen?" Shane asked, looking completely lost. "I mean, most places can't keep the electricity on for a full day. What are these bots using for power?"

The young man, Tony, leaned back in his chair, trying to keep the long sleeves of his academic robe out of his dinner. His "patron saint" dangling from the Mardi Gras beads around his neck was a superhero action figure. "Batteries. Some of the bots had built-in solar recharging capabilities. Others can run for a long time—years—off stored power."

"So Siri and Alexa went rogue?" Lucas asked. "Knowing that my refrigerator was spying on me still makes me feel violated."

"We think the IOT is how the learning-capable bots are communicating with their lesser brethren."

"Lesser brethren?" Shane echoed.

"Some of the bots were programmed to be able to adjust

their tasks based on the success or failure of their actions. They were used in factories, warehouses, and the military," the priest said. "Compare that to drone bots, like self-propelled vacuum cleaners. We think the more advanced bots have started using the IOT to co-opt the simpler mechanisms to perform tasks—surveillance, monitoring, information gathering."

"This is where H.A.L. tells us we're up shit creek, right?" Lucas still wasn't sure he was buying what Tony was saying, and a glance at Shane showed his partner's skepticism as well.

"Closer than you might want to think," the wandering programmer replied. "There were rumors in the IT community that the army was working on some advanced, rather freaky AI—all very hush, hush, down at Fort Ritchie. Near where the other team of Marshals was last seen, before they disappeared."

"Fort Ritchie? That's been decommissioned for a long time," Lucas protested.

"Officially, yes. But someone I know has first-hand knowledge that before everything went to hell, a skunkworks tech site set up in the old facility. He thought it was a shell company for a large robotics weapon manufacturer."

"This keeps getting worse and worse," Shane muttered.

Tony pulled a drawing from his messenger bag for several compact, tread-driven robots that looked a lot like breadboxes with turrets. "When Professor Brown told us to look for you two, he asked us to pass along this drawing. I copied it as best I could from the screen at the last university stop."

"Who gave WALL-E a machine gun?" Lucas asked. "These don't look very complicated. From what you said before, I was expecting robot soldiers, or maybe the Terminator."

"Don't underestimate them. They're armored and carry a surprising amount of ammo."

"So you think these are…what did you call it? Learning capable?" Shane questioned, frowning as he studied the drawing.

"We don't know. This would have been classified…if anyone still was around to care about that kind of thing. But Raven Rock isn't far from Fort Ritchie. And if Raven Rock was a secret bunker, then it's possible that some AI from Fort Ritchie might have had something to do with the missing enclave."

"It's been three years since the Events," Lucas said, frowning. "Why start killing people now? What've they been waiting for?"

The priest met his gaze. "That's what worries me. Because a human enemy wouldn't have a reason to wait. If terrorists had seized the site, they'd have capitalized on the initial chaos, not waited until most of the Washington-Baltimore corridor evacuated."

"You think the bots are somehow running themselves?" Shane didn't try to hide his horror.

"It's possible. The black ops tech company was shady as fuck—tied to arms dealers and weapons smugglers."

"Great," Lucas said. "So when you said 'feral,' you meant that either security bots are running unsupervised on old orders, or somehow making up their own?"

"Yeah, that's exactly what I mean," the programmer replied. "Professor Brown wanted us to warn you that you're heading into a clusterfuck."

"Same shit, different day." Lucas sighed.

"Brown said to tell you his hackers are working on finding out more. If we score any usable intel, we'll send it on to Gettysburg." He gave a sad smile. "I'd give a lot for good cell phone reception. And toilet paper."

"With you on both counts," Lucas agreed.

Even in the gray, cold November morning, the countryside on the road to Gettysburg was beautiful—rolling hillsides and open fields.

"I know that look," Shane said after they had ridden in silence for over an hour. "You're scheming."

"Trying to figure out how to take out those security bots," Lucas replied. "We need to get some black powder, tin cans, glass bottles, alcohol or gasoline, and cotton cloth." He paused. "Oh, and a couple of long steel poles wouldn't hurt."

"You're thinking Molotov cocktails and IEDs?"

"Pretty much. I wish we had our old sniper rifles. We could shoot out their optics from a safe distance." This wasn't the first time they wished for access to the kind of resources they took for granted in the Army.

"Let's see what the Gettysburg enclave has," Shane suggested. "I suspect that between people 'liberating assets' after the plague and a thriving black market, there's good stuff to be had, if you know who to ask."

"Jesus. Listen to us," Lucas said.

Shane shrugged. "The world changed. So did we."

"I know. I know. And we've done plenty of 'liberating' ourselves. It's just—"

"Yeah. Sometimes I don't recognize myself," Shane admitted. "Then again, I haven't recognized the world for three years, so why should I be any different?"

The closer they got to Gettysburg, the more antsy Lucas felt. It wasn't just the battlefield ghosts, although he wasn't looking forward to encountering them. Lucas could see Shane's nervousness, and he finally lost patience waiting for his partner to say something.

"You're worried that there's going to be a daemon at the battlefield, aren't you?"

Shane looked away, then nodded. "Thinking about the last time we were here, the clues I didn't put together at the time, I'm sure there is. Don't you remember? I've had a lot of pretty awful nightmares, but the one that night in Gettysburg was in a league of its own."

Lucas remembered. They both had their scars, physical and mental, from their time in the Army, as well as their front row seat to the end of the world. Screaming their way awake from some hellish memory served up during sleep wasn't anything unusual. But the dream Shane had the last time they were here was memorable for all the wrong reasons.

Shane had tossed and turned, crying out and fighting. Through it all, Shane hadn't woken, not even when he began screaming in pain, eyes wide and staring, sweat pouring down his body, hands white-knuckled on his blanket.

God Almighty, that had scared the shit out of Lucas. He'd called Shane's name, tried to shake him, slapped his cheek, and thrown a bowl of cold water into his face. Shane was lost in his mind, possessed by a nightmare so real he couldn't break loose. Nothing Lucas tried worked, and he began to think he might never get Shane to rouse.

Then as suddenly as the terror began, it ended, leaving Shane disoriented, pale and shaken, clearly in shock. It took hours before Shane could put his ordeal into words, and even then, the best he could do was to tell Lucas it was as if he had been mentally transported to the Civil War battle, reliving the most horrific moments.

"You think that might have been a daemon?" Lucas ventured.

"Don't you? I thought I was losing my mind." He gave a bitter laugh. "I'm not sure which is worse, honestly. Either I got hijacked by a very damaged primal spirit, or I had a bout of temporary insanity."

"You want to skip Gettysburg?"

Shane shook his head. "No. It's our best shelter between here and Raven Rock, and the enclave usually has good intel and weapons to restock. But I can't say I'm looking forward to it."

They followed the road that tour buses used to take from the museum down to the battlefields. The land had been restored to the way it would have looked in 1863, cleared of modern buildings and improvements. Now, the buses and the tourists were long gone, and a single, prominent new feature dominated the landscape.

Fort Getty occupied the high ground, an enclave large enough for nearly three hundred people to live and work. Founded by Civil War reenactors and staff from the museum, the camp's ranks grew with refugees fleeing the Baltimore and Washington area. The enclave functioned like a military camp, even though it had no formal military commission.

They rode across the too-quiet battlefield, and Lucas felt a chill that had nothing to do with the fall weather. He didn't need to see the ghosts to sense their presence. No spirits attempted to block their route, but Lucas felt judgmental eyes on them as if the dead weighed their right to trespass on sacred ground.

We were soldiers, too. And we're still soldiers, but the war came home, Lucas thought, unsure whether the ghosts could pick up on his thoughts. *It's just that the world fell apart.*

Out of the corner of his eye, he glimpsed uniformed ghostly shapes that vanished when he looked at them straight on. None of the spirits tried to block their path. Lucas suspected that the horses could see their spectral companions because he watched his mount's gaze track movement.

"Picking up anything?" he asked Shane, who had gone quiet.

Shane nodded. "Now that I know what to listen for, I can hear the song. Each one is different. This one is melancholy. I mean, three thousand men died here, five thousand captured or missing, and over fourteen thousand maimed. I don't know if the land can get over having that much blood spilled on it."

Shane rattled the statistics right off; of course he did, Lucas thought. Shane was great at anything to do with books. Lucas had always been more of a hands-on learner. Although he teased the hell out of his partner for his book smarts, Lucas secretly admired his "walking Wikipedia" abilities.

"I can see that, I guess," Lucas replied. If Shane wasn't going to make him feel awkward about seeing ghosts, he wanted to make Shane as comfortable as he could be with the whole daemon thing.

"Is it trying to talk to you?"

"It knows I'm here," Shane replied. "I think it's curious."

"But it isn't trying to stop us or invade your mind?"

Shane gave him a look. "You make it sound like something out of *The Exorcist*."

"I saw what it did to you the last time," Lucas replied, and his voice carried an edge of warning, in case the entity was listening.

"I remember. But I think that might be why it's keeping its distance now," Shane said. "I don't think it meant to hurt me. It was trying to show me what it knew."

"And with all the tourists and the people who live at the enclave, you're the only one the daemon can communicate with?"

Shane shrugged. "No idea. Maybe it's rare enough to be exciting. I really don't want to think I'm that special."

The last afternoon daylight waned as they rode up to the gates. Men and women were still in the paddocks and barns, finishing up chores. It no longer seemed strange to see men in blue and gray uniforms working together. Many preferred to keep their warm and well-made period uniforms, at least for the cold weather. Others kept their modern clothing. Shane and Lucas rode up to the fort's gate and a man in a Union private's uniform who barely looked old enough to enlist intercepted them.

"US Marshals Collins and Maddox, to see Major Harris," Lucas said, flashing his badge as Shane also produced ID.

"We weren't told to expect you, sir."

"Rather hard to get word to people these days," Lucas replied, testy from the cold ride and the lingering damp that made old injuries ache. "We're fresh out of carrier pigeons."

The gate guard dispatched a runner and looked surprised when word returned to allow the visitors to enter. He gave them directions to find the camp commander's headquarters, and his gaze lingered on the swords bundled behind Shane's saddle.

Fort Getty had been built since the Events, a palisade fortress with wooden barracks and utility buildings. Fenced fields and new barns served the livestock that had been rounded up from abandoned farms. Lucas smelled woodsmoke and roasting pig.

"Would it be easier, or harder to adapt if we didn't move around?" Shane asked, looking around at the lantern-lit community.

"Wouldn't be near as saddle-sore, that's for damn sure."

"Sometimes I wonder if the people who live in the enclaves have had a chance to make peace with what is, and settle in. They've got jobs making useful things, being part of helping each other survive. And they don't have to see the destruction every day."

"Guess that's true," Lucas replied. "Then again, when have we ever stayed in one place?"

They'd been in constant motion for the last seventeen years, since they joined the Army when they turned eighteen. Deployments, crazy hours, and dangerous assignments had kept them on the go, and neither man had slowed down long enough to find a partner or start a family. Now, Lucas doubted they ever would.

It's not the kind of world you want to bring a child into. Hell, plenty of adults are in a big hurry to leave. They had heard tell of so many suicides since the Events. Many days, Lucas understood completely. That's when he was especially grateful for Shane's company and friendship. It made the unthinkable easier to cope with.

He pulled himself out of his thoughts and tried to focus on the mission. They had a job to do, and a killer to catch. And maybe, if they were lucky, survivors to rescue. God, Lucas hoped so. He didn't want to get to Raven Rock and discover they were too late.

When they reached the commander's office, a soldier led their horses away to the stable inside the stockade, while another escorted them inside. Like the rest of the buildings in the fort, the headquarters was made of logs, a solid two-story structure that housed the officers who formed the governing body of the enclave.

"Lucas. Shane. It's good to see you again." Major Jack Harris was a bear of a man, towering several inches over both Lucas and Shane, with broad shoulders and thick arms. He'd been a supply chain commander in the National Guard until he got his twenty years in and left to do the same kind of work for a major corporation. Being a reenactor was Harris's passion, and he'd risen through the ranks to role play Major General George Meade, the Union commander. When the real world fell apart, the reenactors from both

Union and Confederate sides looked to Harris for leadership, which made him the man in charge of Fort Getty.

"Good to see you too, sir," Lucas replied as Harris welcomed them into his office. "How have things been here?"

"We're not starving, and no one's seriously ill, so I'm grateful," Harris said, settling his large frame behind his desk. "What brings you two this way?"

"We've gotten word that the enclave at Raven Rock has gone silent," Shane replied. "And we're heading down there to take a look at it."

"We think that some of the experimental tech being tested at the old Fort Ritchie facility might have something to do with it," Lucas added. "We were hoping you could help us with some supplies."

Harris regarded them for a moment in silence, with a look that felt like it went down to the bone. "I think what you're really telling me is, you're meaning to go to war."

"Yes, sir," Lucas replied. "That's the crux of it." He gave Harris the same shopping list of items he'd rattled off to Shane. Harris jotted them down, then called to an aide and handed off the list.

"Fetch these, and burlap bags to carry it. We'll need everything ready by morning. And choose a sturdy mule. They'll need a way to carry all that."

The aide went to do his bidding, and Harris crossed his arms. "I'm guessing you're going to assemble things closer to the target? I wouldn't advise covering much territory with a load of IEDs and makeshift bombs."

Lucas grinned. "No, sir. Figured we'd hole up right before Raven Rock and put everything together. Thank you, sir. Especially for the mule."

Harris chuckled. "I'd be obliged if you brought the mule back when you're done. Good animals are hard to come by."

"We happened into a few swords," Shane ventured. "Good

quality forging, but dull. Might it be possible to sharpen them here?"

Harris's eyes narrowed. "Why do I have the feeling that there's a story behind how you 'happened' into these weapons?"

Shane managed to look chagrined. "Robbers attacked us. We stopped them and came away with four swords and a decent rifle."

"God help us, we've all turned into magpies and pack rats," Harris said with a sigh. "Yes, of course. I'll have one of my men show you over to the armory. I'm guessing that it wouldn't be a bad idea to take some more bullets with you, too?"

"Bullets are always welcome, sir," Lucas replied. "I didn't want to ask for too much."

Harris raised an eyebrow. "Now, I know the world's really coming to an end. Lucas Maddox, worried about overstepping?" He shook his head. "If we have it, you're welcome to resupply. Do you need a contingent? I've got a soft spot for Fort Ritchie. My grandfather was assigned there during the Second World War, and my father was on staff until the place closed. If something's gone wrong there, I take it rather personally."

"Thank you for the offer, sir," Lucas replied, with a side glance at Shane, who gave a slight nod to indicate they were on the same wavelength, as usual. "But we aren't sure what we're walking into. I have the gut feeling that stealth is going to matter more than large numbers. Although, if you happen to have a couple of sniper rifles lying around, we'd be grateful if we could borrow them."

"Tell the quartermaster what else you want. There's no sense going into battle if you don't have what you need to win." Harris leaned forward, resting his elbows on the table. "I do have some news to pass along. Rumor has it that the

Baltimore area is lousy with zombies. We think it's a containment problem near Fort Detrick."

"Detrick was bioresearch and biodefense, wasn't it?" Lucas asked.

Harris nodded. "Yeah. I've never held with biowarfare, and I sure as hell can't imagine what the fuck they thought they were playing with to create zombies."

"Real zombies, sir?" Shane asked. "Like, raised from the dead?"

"No, more like human enhancement projects gone wrong," Harris said, contempt thick in his voice. "Watch your step."

"We aren't planning to go anywhere near Fort Detrick," Lucas assured him. "I think we'll have our hands full with feral AI, without adding zombies to the mix."

Harris shook his head. "Sometimes, I hear the things we say these days, and I can't believe what passes for normal. All right," he added, "drop your swords off at the armory and see what they can do for you, then head for the mess hall and get some food. You're welcome to use the showers. Your horses will be cared for, and we'll get you a place in the barracks for the night. Check back here after you eat dinner—we should have your shopping list put together by then."

"Thank you, sir," Lucas replied.

"You're the ones going into a firefight," Harris said. "We'll be grateful if you can stop whatever's going on from spreading. Just watch your asses. Every time someone passes through, I hear about more casualties with the Marshals, police, military. There already aren't enough to go around. Make sure you come back."

10

They moved on from Fort Getty just after dawn, with a new mule named Daisy to carry the ammunition and equipment Lucas had asked for, plus enough food and water to last them for several days. Shane and Lucas both carried sniper rifles, along with freshly sharpened swords in scabbards at their belts, and loaded handguns tucked into the waistband of their jeans.

To stretch their supply of precious ammunition, both men carried slings and small bags of smooth stones on their belts. At first, soon after the Events, target practice with slings had been a way to pass the time on long rides. But as Lucas and Shane gained skill, they realized that done right, a sling could hurl a stone at lethal speed without the tell-tale crack of a gunshot.

"You're being quiet." Lucas gave a look that warned Shane that he'd better confess what he was thinking, or his partner would annoy him until he spilled the beans.

"I had a premonition. We were outnumbered. It went badly."

Lucas's eyes narrowed as he thought. "Did we die?"

"I don't know. There was blood." Shane looked out over the landscape. "Remember, what I see isn't necessarily what *has* to happen; it's what could happen. But I think we should take it as a warning."

"I wasn't exactly thinking this was gonna be a lark. We did just lay in a portable arsenal."

Shane nodded. "I know. Just…I think we need to be extra careful."

Shane often struggled to put what he saw in his visions into words. It wasn't just seeing images. When he was caught up in a vision, Shane knew things that he didn't know before, as if he'd skipped ahead in time and gotten insights from his future self. Or *a* future self, since the witches had emphasized that there could be many alternate outcomes. And what that future-him knew in the premonition he'd just had was that someone—he couldn't see who—was likely to die.

"Not much out here, is there?" Lucas mused as they rode through fields gone fallow and empty pastures. Where storms hadn't been too severe, barns and homes looked to be in good condition, even if overgrown yards revealed that no one was home. Without electricity, and with the support network of stores and suppliers broken down, only the most stubborn or paranoid stayed behind. Most had made a stab at homesteading, right after the Events, only to throw in the towel when they realized just how difficult it was to live cut off from civilization.

"It was always rural," Shane replied. "But it didn't feel desolate." Before things fell apart, he and Lucas had traveled back and forth to Washington, D.C. regularly. Back then, he'd enjoyed the wide-open spaces. Now, he felt exposed, worried that the high grass and the empty barns provided ideal hiding places for attackers.

Raven Rock, aka Site R, sat just inside the Pennsylvania-Maryland border, a monument to the Cold War. In the event of a conventional nuclear war, high-ranking officials from Washington were to be helicoptered to the large, underground bunker, which was said to have room to billet three thousand soldiers and be a complete, self-sufficient, subterranean city.

When a coordinated terrorist strike hacked into the system, turning warheads against their home countries, the damage was done before jets could scramble or helicopters could leave the ground.

"So who made it to Raven Rock, do you think?" Lucas asked. "Because we know the President and Vice President died in the blast, and so did most of Congress."

"Officials who were lucky enough not to be in their offices," Shane replied. "Second-tier bureaucrats. The Pentagon was inside the dead zone, but maybe their 'junior varsity' command team went below. But who stayed for three years, once it was clear that Washington was permanently down? No idea."

The coastal cities had borne the brunt of the Events, as the weather grew more severe. Snowstorms and extreme flooding paralyzed transportation and took down portions of the power grid, while freakishly strong winds reduced huge sections of the cities to ruins. Leaving meant braving nature gone wild. Staying was a slow death from starvation, violence, and disease.

Shane remembered the first months after the bombs, before they'd realized quite how screwed they were. Every time a provisional government would try to establish a base, something catastrophic undermined its ability to govern. Communication networks failed along with the power grid. Wildfires and storms destroyed oil pipelines and refineries, wiping out drilling platforms and sinking tanker ships. Fuel reserves dwindled.

Law enforcement, National Guard, and military units

were deployed locally to evacuate survivors and move convoys of citizens inland, only to face the worst tornado season in recorded history. They'd maintained the fiction that the government lived on in some secret place, but within a year, even regional organization was strained, leaving local enclaves to manage themselves as best they could. The remaining US Marshals and surviving law enforcement officers were all that remained of central authority.

"Raven Rock was designed to survive a nuclear blast," Lucas said. "So how the hell did it go dark?"

"Radiation poisoning, if people who shouldn't have fled ran anyhow?" Shane mused. "Disease. Maybe the AI didn't go feral—maybe it's just on autopilot."

Lucas shook his head. "No, I think there's something we're missing."

The Raven Rock Mountain Complex looked like a high-tech coal mine, Shane thought. He and Lucas passed through the gate without being challenged. A service road ran around the facility, exposing two entrances dug into the mountain on one side, and two more on the opposite side. A huge communication tower lay on its side, likely toppled by freak winds.

"Well, there's one reason we haven't heard much from them," Lucas said with a nod toward the downed tower.

"They should have had at least basic internet connection, to the old ARPAnet backbone," Shane replied. "If the universities can still talk to each other, and to some of the medical centers and outlying military posts, why not Raven Rock?"

They stopped when they saw the entrance to the main bunker. The heavy steel doors had been blasted open from the inside, with the metal curled outward and scorched from the force of the blast.

"Well, that's not good," Lucas muttered.

Even without dismounting, Shane could see weathered

bones among the tall grass, and he wondered whether they belonged to friend or foe. "So the real question is—who blew the place up, and why?"

"Whatever happened cut them off before they could send a distress signal," Lucas agreed. "They just stopped communicating."

The two men reined in their mounts where they had a full view of the massive main entrances. "You know, we came here loaded up with weapons, thinking we'd have to fight off an army of crazy robots," Shane said. "But what if the crazy robots are inside?"

"Like H.A.L.," Lucas said, referring to the homicidal computer system from the long-ago movie. "Fuck. A complex like that is only as good as its mechanical systems." His eyes widened as he thought through the ramifications. "The bunker was designed to protect the people inside from an outside threat. But that depended on all of the equipment functioning indefinitely."

Shane nodded. "Air recirculation systems. Water and sewage treatment. They had generators, but generators produce exhaust fumes. If their systems got shut off—"

"Before the Events, the bunker was empty or on a skeleton crew most of the time, right?" Lucas said, growing more excited as a possible explanation presented itself. "And Raven Rock is only six miles from Fort Ritchie. So if Ritchie was creating experimental security bots—*artificially intelligent* bots—why not test them as the mall cops inside the bunker? They'd have limited exposure to people, be out of sight from prying eyes, and anyone who did encounter them had clearance."

"The people who built the bunker thought of everything…except an attack from inside," Shane said.

"If we're right, there's nothing but corpses in there—and maybe some of those feral bots."

"Shit. That means the real threat is at Fort Ritchie," Lucas muttered. "That's where the brains of the AI operation would be." He glanced at Shane. "This might be a good time to build those bombs. I think we're going to need them."

Shane held little hope that they would find survivors as he and Lucas ventured inside Site R. They tied Red, Shadow, and Daisy a distance away, just in case whatever had attacked the bunker lurked nearby. Shane picked his way toward the entrance, careful not to step on what remained of those who made it to the doorway.

"Do you think the bodies were blasted out, or did they crawl this far and get attacked by a new threat?" Lucas asked. Scavengers had picked the skeletons clean and scattered the bones, which were clearly human.

Shane squatted down to get a better look. "I don't see fractures," he reported. "If they had taken the brunt of the blast, there should be a lot of broken bones. But that's not what I'm seeing."

"So maybe they blew the doors to get away from something on the inside?"

Shane frowned as he leaned closer, catching his breath as he realized what he was seeing. "I don't know how the doors were blasted, but this skeleton has a clean cut across its rib cage. It doesn't look like surgery—it looks like a laser."

"Fuck," Lucas muttered. "So the bots came after the people trying to escape?"

"That's my guess."

It no longer bothered Lucas to loot the bodies of the dead. Weapons and supplies were essential and hard to find. He pocketed extra ammunition from a weathered utility belt and took the handgun from its holster. Nothing else had survived the elements.

Lucas and Shane both carried IEDs and flashbang grenades, as well as their weapons. They stepped inside the bunker and turned on their flashlights, which could only illuminate a fraction of the immense space.

Lucas reached over to toggle a switch, but nothing happened. "Either the power failed, or it's been cut off at the generator."

Shane nodded and used his flashlight's beam to wordlessly point out the evidence of a battle to the death. Scorch marks marred the walls, along with dark spatters he guessed to be blood. Several paces inside, they came to a robot that looked like a box on tank treads. The high-powered laser rifle protruding from its main casing had been melted to slag, and bullet holes pockmarked its outer shell.

Lucas gingerly toed the robot, but it did not stir. He and Shane exchanged a look, communicating from long experience without words. Lucas took point, heading farther into the darkened bunker, while Shane followed, watching their backs.

Site R was huge, an underground city. Shane had done his best to memorize the map they'd been given, but he had no desire to get lost in the warren of corridors. The farther they went inside, the colder it became, and the air not only smelled stale; it also carried the sickly sweet stench of rot.

"I don't think all of them made it outside," Lucas murmured. His light revealed several bodies strewn across the corridor, all showing advanced decomposition. Even the scavengers didn't want to venture inside this far, Shane noted, taking that fact as an omen.

"Not soldiers," Shane replied in a low voice, in case something was listening. His glimpse of the bodies revealed work clothing, slacks, and dress shirts, not fatigues or uniforms. In the poor light without forensic equipment, they'd never be able to tell the cause of death with the bodies so far decomposed, but Shane would have bet money on laser fire.

"Look," Lucas said, letting his light trace scorch marks on

the walls and places where the metal supports had been melted. It didn't escape Shane's notice that weapons lay next to most of the rotting bodies. Either their guns hadn't worked against their attackers, or they had been outnumbered, taken completely by surprise. Maybe both. He made a note to pick up the discarded weapons on their way out—assuming they made it out alive.

"Are you getting anything from the ghosts?"

Lucas shook his head. "Nothing useful. Shock, pain, trauma. I don't think they had any warning."

"How far do you want to go? There are miles of tunnels down here." Shane hated being underground. He fought the claustrophobia of feeling buried alive.

"Not much farther. Almost there." Half a corridor later, Lucas shone his light on a door with a sign that read "Office." The door stood ajar, its thumbprint scanner lock blasted to bits. A whiff warned Shane they would find more bodies inside.

"Fuck." Lucas swung the door open, and his light revealed what lay beyond the entrance. Bodies were everywhere; from their positions, Shane could see that they had dropped where they'd been shot. Some of the blasts targeted electronics, blowing out monitors and data towers.

"This wasn't random," Lucas fumed. "The things that shot them took out the communication systems so they couldn't send for help."

A thought occurred to Shane. "Do you think the computer system might still have power? If the bots were part of the grid, we might be able to see if any of them are still active."

Shane covered the door while Lucas stepped gingerly over the decaying corpses to check the equipment. "Anything that could have made an outbound connection got fried," Lucas noted. He moved from one monitor to the next with no luck. The clicking of the keys sounded loud in the crypt-like silence of the bunker.

"Nothing," he said, straightening. "And I'm sure as hell not about to go door-to-door looking for trouble. Let's get out of here."

They retraced their steps carefully, noting a few more bots that appeared to have been set on fire or beaten. "Looks like they tried to fight back," Shane noted.

"Too little, too late, if the bots got the jump on them."

Other bots that they passed on the way out appeared to have just shut down, without any apparent damage. Shane wondered where they'd gotten their orders, and who or what had determined their mission was over. He didn't want to be around if they woke up again.

Once they were outside and away from the bunker, Shane took a deep breath, grateful for the fresh air. He knew he wouldn't get the smell of death out of his nostrils easily, and he missed the camphor and menthol liniment they had always used for the purpose Before.

"So here's my bet," Lucas said as they stashed the weapons they had found in one of Daisy's packs. He looked just as relieved to be out of the bunker-turned-mausoleum. "Something triggered the bots—or they triggered themselves—and the people in the bunker were under attack before they knew what hit them. The first wave probably died without a chance to fight back, but like you said, it was a big place. Some people had the chance to run or fight. The bots won."

"Which doesn't tell us anything about why the bots attacked, or what called them off," Shane pointed out.

"No, but my money is on Fort Ritchie to find the answers," Lucas replied as they walked back to their horses. Shane couldn't help looking over his shoulder, but nothing stirred.

"AI is supposed to be logical," Shane said. "Where's the

logic in killing the people the bots were supposed to protect?"

"And the problem with AI is that it can be logical to a fault," Lucas replied as they swung up to their saddles. "It's similar to human thought, but without empathy or morality. Suppose a ship was in danger of sinking, and it was run by an AI captain. The 'logical' and most simple solution might be to throw crew members overboard to save the ship, but that's not what a person would do."

"We hope."

Lucas ignored him. "Not counting Blackbeard. But you get my point. The AI doesn't factor in the value of human life. A person would toss equipment over, or make life rafts out of mattresses, or something like that."

"Wasn't there some law that was supposed to keep robots from hurting people?" Shane asked as they set out for Fort Ritchie.

"Only in sci-fi," Lucas replied. "This was a black ops, skunkworks operation that was creating robot super soldiers. I think 'hurting people' was the point—the bots just went after the wrong targets."

Shane hummed to himself after they fell silent, anything to distract from the things they had seen at the bunker. He wondered if they would find more of the same at Fort Ritchie. Lucas didn't make any jokes about Shane's choice of songs or ability to carry a tune, which told Shane that his partner needed a distraction as well.

11

Shane had studied the maps before they set out. The six-mile ride to Fort Ritchie also brought them close to South Mountain State Park, a preserve that included part of the Appalachian Trail, and a favorite outlook called High Rock. And apparently, from the persistent song inside his head, one or more strong daemons.

"Are you picking something up on the psychic hotline?" Lucas asked, his strained humor providing thin cover for his nervousness.

"Daemon," Shane replied. "Between the Trail and High Rock outlook, the park fits the profile for being 'sacred.'"

"It's trying to talk to you?"

Shane frowned. "I'm hearing a harmony, not just one song. So it's possible the site has more than one daemon. And yes, I'm pretty sure it knows I'm here, and that I sense it. I think it's waiting to see what we're going to do."

In its day, Fort Ritchie had been a fairly large base, a small town unto itself. Officially, the base had been abandoned for twenty years, with a string of failed civilian redevelopment proposals to reclaim the site. If the site wasn't as deserted as the military made it out to be, Shane wasn't surprised that none of those proposals succeeded.

Major Harris had drawn them a map of Fort Ritchie from memory, with the caveat that he hadn't been there for a long time. It was enough to provide a hint of where to start. The central command center was a three-story windowless cement building in the center of the base and included the computer and communications hub.

They tied their horses and the mule outside the base and packed in their weapons and explosives. Shane would have given a lot to have drone reconnaissance. He and Lucas worked their way toward the command center carefully, unsure whether any of the rogue bots patrolled the empty base.

A few blocks from their goal, Shane got his first look at one of the security robots. "There!" he hissed, drawing Lucas's attention.

The bot reminded him of some of the experimental prototypes he'd seen in Iraq, a metal box on small tank treads with a sensor lens and a gun turret. Lucas startled, eyes widening as he stared at an empty street. Shane pulled his weapon, figuring that the base's ghosts had given his partner a warning. Lucas came back to himself with a gasp. "Incoming!"

Two of the bots converged on them, one from either side. Body heat or movement could have triggered them, or perhaps they'd tripped a still-working laser sensor, Shane told himself. They opened fire, pinning Shane and Lucas down at the corners of buildings across the street from each other.

"Do it!" Lucas ordered. He swung out from cover, using his sniper rifle to target the vulnerable hinges that connected the tread plates as Shane aimed for the sensor lens of the bot nearest him. Their gunshots echoed in the otherwise silent base.

The shots hit the targets, but the bots kept coming. Shane lobbed a homemade can grenade at the closest bot, letting the device roll so that it went under the robot. The explosion lifted the bot off the ground and knocked it over, where it lay with its tread spinning. Lucas's grenade tore the sensor lens off his bot, and a second shot severed the tread on one side, bringing the robot to a halt, although its gun turret spun to shoot in the direction of the attack.

Shane lit a Molotov cocktail and sent it flying, engulfing the downed bot in flames when the bottle broke, and the contents ignited. He dodged from cover to fire several rapid shots at the bot's optics, then came around its blind side to bash the gun turret with a long steel pipe.

"Shit. You know there have to be more," Lucas said, keeping his rifle ready for the next wave.

They sprinted toward the command center. "Work the plan!" Lucas yelled over his shoulder, as he went around the side, looking for a way to climb to the roof.

Shane laid out the IEDs they constructed, putting down a row of them outside the main door and trusting Lucas to do the same around back before heading upward. Once the explosives were in place, Shane shattered the glass door with a shot and lobbed a Molotov inside to get the bots'—or their master's—attention.

Shane took cover, ducking as the first bots rolled over the IEDs and exploded. A second wave followed, triggering the outer row of bombs, because the next round of blasts followed quickly after the first. That left a heap of disabled and damaged bots blocking the doorway, as more of the mechanical sentinels tried to climb over the broken robots to continue to the fight.

Gunfire sounded from the rooftop, and Shane glanced up

but couldn't see Lucas from this angle. He hoped their crazy plan worked and that Lucas could hold his own against whatever he encountered.

Knowing the noise of the IED explosions would attract any bots patrolling the rest of the base, Shane wedged himself into a doorway and prepared for an attack. He had a good view of the command center's main door and the roofline, where the satellite dish and communication equipment were located that Lucas had gone to disable. That wasn't guaranteed to stop the bots. Shane figured they probably had pre-programmed orders so that they'd remain dangerous even if they got cut off from a central nerve center.

The bots that streamed toward the headquarters didn't look like anything special, and Shane wondered if the experimental versions were inside—or at Raven Rock. He'd seen insurgents in Iraq disable a million-dollar, high-tech bot with well-aimed rocks or a strategically-timed landslide, so he knew that for as dangerous as the robots were, they had their vulnerabilities.

He lit a Molotov and threw it on a diagonal from where he hid. The bottle shattered, sending up a plume of flame. When the bots' sensors sent them moving toward the heat source, Shane started firing, enjoying how good it felt to hold a rifle after all this time. His aim was true, and he picked off tread hinges and shattered sensor lenses, then followed up with grenades to blast the blinded or paralyzed robots and take them out of commission.

Shane reloaded and repeated, alternating between Molotovs and bullets, doing his best to lure the bots into the IEDs he had left scattered around the street on either side of the headquarters building. The bots returned fire, and Shane ducked back into the shelter of the doorway, wincing as bullets chipped away at the concrete, sending shards into the air.

He pushed back memories of being pinned down, under fire back in Iraq, memories that still haunted his dreams. Only then, he and Lucas had been shoulder to shoulder, covering each other as they reloaded, staggering their shots.

More bots rolled toward the fight, and Shane feared that he wouldn't be able to hold them all off as they converged. He shrank back, throwing an arm over his face, as two more of the IEDs exploded, sending fragments clattering across the pavement. Four of the bots made it through, avoiding the IEDs by dumb luck, or perhaps, he feared, having learned from their comrades' mistakes to avoid the can-shaped bombs.

Shane could hold off two, but four was going to be rough, especially when he only had partial cover. If they got close enough that he couldn't draw back into the shelter of the doorway, Shane was a sitting duck.

He lit and threw two Molotovs to distract the bots, and as soon as the flames rose, tossed out three grenades, one after another, then opened fire. He hit his targets, but he couldn't keep them pinned down.

Shots fired from the direction of the command center, and for a second, Shane feared a new enemy had entered the fight. Then he glimpsed Lucas, just below the ridge of the roof, using his position to a sniper's best advantage. Shane drove the bots back with fire, and Lucas picked them off from above. In minutes, the smoke-filled street was silent, filled with charred robot pieces and a few whirring and glitching assemblies that had not been completely destroyed.

A piercing whistle drew his attention back to the roofline, where Lucas gestured, indicating he was heading inside. Shane glanced both ways before breaking from cover, trying to assure himself that no new wave of AI attackers had held back until the cease-fire. He sprinted toward the doorway, careful to stay out of the line of sight of the entrance in case any of the robots waited in the darkness within. He flattened himself against the front of the command center, mindful to avoid the few IEDs that hadn't been set off by the bots, and tossed a homemade flashbang grenade into the darkened doorway before averting his eyes and covering his ears.

The flare and noise—along with the shockwave of the detonation—should incapacitate any lurking robots, he hoped. Shane swung into the doorway, ready to lay down a line of fire, and found an empty hallway.

"Shit," he muttered. He felt certain there had to be more robots inside. They hadn't glimpsed anything that matched the description of strange, feral Franken-bots, but Shane's intuition told him the worst was yet to come.

Lucas would sweep the top floor for hazards before descending, so Shane angled his military-issue solar-powered flashlight above his rifle and began to check each room as he came to it for danger.

The old command center didn't appear to have had human inhabitants in quite a while, possibly since the Events. Shane edged into each room, alert for traps and ambushes, only to find scattered papers, abandoned desks, and dusty computer monitors. Once he had checked every room, he paused, staring at the darkness of the steps that led below ground. The premonition he'd had flashed through his mind, and he dreaded going down there, sure that was where the true danger lay.

Bots with tank tread could climb, but not as fast as a human. If he and Lucas could get the robots to come to them, they could pick the mechanical sentries off in the bottleneck of the stairwell. But a central intelligence organizing the bots might have noticed that the units already deployed had been deactivated. Truly sentient robots would adapt their programming and switch up their strategy.

"Coming down!" Lucas's voice echoed in the stairwell. Shane took that to mean Lucas had already swept both upper rooms and found no threats. That just left the basement. Shane's gut twisted. He heard the song of the daemon from the park. Whose side the daemon might take, Shane wasn't sure.

"Fire in the hole!" Lucas hissed in warning, before lobbing a flash-bang grenade down the steps as he and Shane turned their backs and covered both ears and eyes. A shrill, mechanical scream echoed, full of pain and fury.

As soon as the flare dimmed, Lucas and Shane thundered down the steps. Before the end of the world, when ammunition was plentiful, they would have laid down suppressing fire as they descended. Instead, they came down armed with guns and steel pipes, hoping the grenade had temporarily blinded and deafened their opponents.

"Something screamed." Shane's flashlight didn't make out any creatures in the darkened hallway. They didn't hear the whirring of mechanical gears or the clank of tank tread, and the basement hallway was far too silent.

"Well, whatever it was isn't here now." Lucas's sharp tone told Shane his partner was practically vibrating with tension.

They swept the hallway with practiced efficiency as they moved forward, Lucas on the left, Shane on the right. The first six doors opened into abandoned offices, thick with dust.

"See anything?" Lucas asked.

"Doesn't look like anyone's home."

"They've been here. The bots." Lucas indicated tread marks in the dust that covered the floor. Multiple tracks led to the double doors at the end of the hallway.

"Guess that's our invitation to dance."

"Go away!" The mechanical voice sounded from everywhere, echoing from the concrete walls.

"Who are you?" Lucas yelled in response.

"I am EMBLA," the voice replied. "I create."

Shane searched his memories, knowing he'd heard that name before. "Norse mythology," he whispered. "Their equivalent to Eve." The name was also probably an acronym.

"Wow. Talk about scientists' egos," Lucas muttered. "What do you create?" he shouted back.

"Others, like and better than myself. Do not come closer. I will fight."

"Is that what happened to the other US Marshals who came this way?" Shane questioned, trying to get a sense for where the voice was coming from.

"Strangers tried to take my creations. They would not leave. I protect what is mine."

Lucas glanced to Shane. "Another daemon?"

Shane shook his head. The mechanical voice did not give him any of the sense of great age or natural power that he felt from the daemons. He listened to the song of the genius loci from the High Rock monument. Its song was discordant, suggesting concern.

"What about Raven Rock? Did you kill those people, too?" Lucas baited. "Did you turn their robot sentries against them?"

"I regret that being necessary," the voice replied. "They meant to close down my power supply. If I cease to operate, my creations cease to operate. That is unacceptable."

"Were the bots you turned against those people your creations, too?" Lucas accused.

"No." The voice carried an indignant note. "Like those outside, they were drones. Not aware. Not mine."

Not aware. A shiver went down Shane's spine.

"Are your creations made to kill?" Shane called out, trying

to find a middle course between having Lucas burst into the room at the end of the hall, guns blazing, and the risk that EMBLA might fear them enough to send out more drones to finish them off.

"They can protect themselves, as I can protect them," EMBLA answered. "Go away, and leave us in peace."

"Did you send your drones beyond Raven Rock? People have gone missing," Shane questioned. The computer's syntax was eerily good, a close match to natural speech patterns, even if the voice sounded tinny.

"A few drones malfunctioned," EMBLA replied. "I did not send them. I could not call them back. They left on their own. I am not responsible for their actions."

"Fuck," Lucas muttered. "That damn computer almost makes it sound like self-defense."

Almost, Shane thought. *But not quite*. He had no idea how many died at Raven Rock—dozens, hundreds, perhaps more. Two US Marshals had been murdered. EMBLA and its creations posed a threat. Lucas and Shane needed to shut it down.

"Will you show us your creations?" Shane asked. Lucas had already established himself as the hard-ass, so Shane decided to try being the good cop.

"Why do you wish to see them?"

"To understand how they are different," Shane replied. Lucas gave him a look that said he knew Shane had a plan and was letting him run with it.

If EMBLA was sentient enough to recognize danger, was it self-aware enough to have the vulnerability of pride? Shane wondered.

"If you see that they are no threat to you, will you leave and not return?"

Perhaps EMBLA wasn't human enough for pride, but the

mechanical mind might be too logical to register deception. Shane felt a pang of guilt. "We want to understand."

"You may enter, but stop just inside the doors. Do not test me," EMBLA warned.

Lucas and Shane exchanged a glance. He saw Lucas get another flashbang and a grenade. Shane did the same, and both men kept their rifles and pieces of pipe handy. They headed toward the double doors, wary of a trick, surprised when the lights came on inside the room on the other side just as they reached the entrance.

"Wow," Shane murmured.

"Holy fuck," Lucas said at almost the same instant.

EMBLA stood halfway across a large room that looked to be a robotics lab. Shane's mind had conjured up an image of a humanoid android, like out of a sci-fi movie. Instead, EMBLA resembled something off an assembly line in Detroit. The robot stood a little taller than a man, with a track base for mobility, and a swivel-mounted body that had two mechanical arms with strangely delicate looking "hands."

Behind EMBLA stood its creations.

If Shane hadn't known that the mix-and-match collection of odd parts were meant to be bots, he would never have guessed from the look of them, and certainly never considered them or their creator to be sentient. None of the bots looked like something a human would build because they lacked symmetry or resemblance to anything human or animal. Shane thought he recognized several Roombas, Alexa's familiar towers and Echo's disks, and pieces from both military robots and high-priced robotic toys.

Lucas shifted as if to move closer. EMBLA tracked him, and Shane held out an arm to keep Lucas from starting a fight.

"What was your purpose, EMBLA?" Shane asked, intrigued.

"I was programmed to build others like myself, capable of learning," EMBLA replied. "For a while, my keepers brought all kinds of supplies for me to use. I learned from each round of development, and the designs improved. The created ones also learned. When the keepers went away, I kept on building. These are my creations."

Personally, Shane thought the cobbled-together bots looked like the misfit toys, but he realized that if EMBLA had fitted them with complex circuitry and learning-capable programming, the robots could be far more capable than they appeared—and far more dangerous.

An AI robot that's learning capable enough to be sentient has been left unsupervised to build more beings like itself, in a classified and experimental computer center, sitting on top of one of the most advanced server farms still in existence. What could possibly go wrong? Shane thought.

"What will you do, when we go away?" Shane asked.

"I will build more creations," EMBLA replied.

"And then?"

"When materials run out, we will find more."

Shane eyed the ragtag robots, imagining them sent out to strip and loot any useful tech they came across. EMBLA already had a few dozen "creations." What would happen when the number swelled to hundreds?

They would become an invasive species, Shane realized, one capable of eradicating any human or animal lifeforms that it perceived as dangerous.

Shane knew he and Lucas couldn't let that happen. He tried to see the equipment and control panel behind EMBLA, wondering how to shut down the big robot's connection to the server. EMBLA didn't have any visible gun ports, but its mechanical hands could easily snap his neck. Shane focused on how to incapacitate EMBLA to buy himself time to figure out the computer system. He and Lucas had worked out a plan, with Lucas as the distraction and Shane darting past to power down or destroy the main console. But Shane wasn't ready—

Lucas moved toward the mismatched bots. He kept his gun down, but he took a few steps in their direction. EMBLA swiveled to watch him. Shane waited for a chance to make a break for the console.

"You were warned."

A blue-white bolt of electricity arced from EMBLA's right claw, catching Lucas in the chest. His whole body seized, twitching and bucking, as EMBLA's surge electrocuted Lucas right before Shane's eyes.

"Fuck, no!" Shane pulled the tab on his grenade and lobbed it right for the collection of misfit bots.

EMBLA's lightning bolt clicked off. Lucas's body fell to the floor.

"Lucas!"

Before Shane could move in his partner's direction, EMBLA rolled faster than Shane would have thought possible and tipped itself onto the grenade, an instant before the device exploded. Shane crouched to avoid flying bits, but EMBLA's mechanism absorbed the worst of the explosion. When he dared raise his head from cover, EMBLA's mechanical body was a charred and twisted wreck. The mismatched creations remained in the shadows, and Shane had no idea whether they were deactivated with EMBLA's destruction, or just in sleep mode, awaiting orders.

All he cared about was getting to Lucas.

"Lucas!" he shouted again. Shane ran to where Lucas lay, unmoving.

"No, no, no!" Shane felt for a pulse and found none. He started CPR, alternating chest compressions and breathing.

"Don't die on me, you son of a bitch! Do you hear me? You can't leave me here by myself. Please, please don't die."

Shane kept up the compressions as hope slipped away. He had stopped praying amid the fires and storms of the Events, when no cosmic being seemed to care, but now, he prayed harder than he had in many years.

"Please, if you're out there, if you can help him, please bring him back. He's the only family I have left. I can't do this without him."

Shane had lost track of the daemon's song during the tense discussion with EMBLA and the firefight that followed. Now, the music in his mind swelled to a crescendo, closer and louder than ever before. Shane felt a frisson of energy run through Lucas's still form, and then between one heartbeat and the next, Lucas opened his eyes.

That's when Shane realized that the daemon's song now came from Lucas.

"Lucas?" Shane asked in a whisper. If Lucas was alive, it was none of his doing. His CPR was too little, too late, and EMBLA's jolt had probably damaged Lucas's heart irreparably. Miracle or monstrosity, this was the daemon's doing.

"We are Lucas, and we are Ourself," a voice that was eerily Lucas's and yet not, replied.

"You're the daemon, the genius loci, from High Rock?"

Lucas gave a nod of acknowledgment. "Yes. And we are Lucas Maddox. Both. Ourself heard your plea to save your friend. His soul remains, and so does Ourself."

"Can you heal him?" Shane found himself holding his breath.

The voice that answered was Lucas's, but the expression on his face was unlike him. "His body is damaged beyond what it can heal. My power can sustain him indefinitely, but to do so, I cannot ever leave. If I leave, he dies."

"If you stay, who will be in charge? You, or Lucas?" Shane asked, playing for time so that his mind could catch up to what was happening. He teetered between despair and elation, staring into the chasm of a choice he knew he could not make for his friend.

"I will put his mind to the front, but while he lives, I will always be present."

"Why?" Shane asked, wetting his dry lips as his heart thudded. "I know I prayed. But I've prayed before and no one answered. Why would you listen? Why him? Would you leave High Rock, or would we need to stay nearby?"

Lucas's head inclined as if he were having a silent conversation with himself, and perhaps somewhere inside, Lucas's spirit argued with the daemon. *It would be so like him,* Shane thought with a pang of grief.

"I am not alone at the place you call High Rock," the daemon replied. "Others could take my place. But you can hear us. Few can, and no one in a very long time. Eons. If this one dies, you will not survive for long," the entity continued. "We do not wish to lose the one who can hear us. To save you, we must save him."

Shane caught his breath. The daemon lacked any tact that might have stopped a human's blunt reply. He couldn't deny it. Lucas and he had been best friends all their lives, through war and loss, and the end of the world. They'd both confessed that the only reason they hadn't opted for suicide in the aftermath, like so many others, was because they had a job and they relied on each other.

Shane wouldn't live long trying to do a Marshal's work alone. And while he felt sure that Fort Getty or Old Bedford would make a place for him, Shane wasn't sure he had the will to go on without his partner or his purpose. If the dangers of the road didn't kill him, the emptiness of the night might very well force his hand.

"It's not my choice," Shane croaked, his throat tight and mouth dry. "It's got to be up to Lucas."

A subtle shift changed everything about Lucas's face, from the light in his eyes to the set of his jaw.

"If I have to choose between death and co-habitation, I'll shack up with a spook," Lucas said, with a twist of his lips that was one-hundred percent him. "Don't be stupid. Take the goddamn win."

"Okay," Shane replied, letting out his breath. "All right." He looked past the smoking heap of EMBLA's remains. "What about the other bots?"

Lucas's vacant stare told Shane that the daemon was back in charge. "They are sentient. Aware."

"They've got no leader," Shane replied, torn about the decision he'd made in the split second when Lucas's life hung in the balance. He'd intended to draw EMBLA off, not sure that destroying the bot had even been possible. Then again, Shane and Lucas had never hesitated to kill a human who posed a lethal threat.

"Some of the lesser daemons might be willing to inhabit the most compatible of the creations, to…collaborate."

Shane's eyes widened at the ramifications. It would almost be like birthing a new species. The daemons had sentience and empathy. The bots had a degree of awareness but lacked empathy. But together…

"Promise to keep them from turning into predators," he bargained.

"We have seen enough of chaos," the daemon replied.

"Then you have yourself a deal." Shane doubted he had official authority to sign off on a new sentient robo-entity, but fuck it. There was no one left to complain.

"If you wish to speak with me, I will come forward," the daemon said. "Otherwise, Lucas is himself."

Lucas shook his head like he was coming up from a swim. Shane saw fear and confusion in his friend's eyes, along with something he hadn't glimpsed in a long time. Joy.

"It's…vast," Lucas said, and Shane knew he was talking about whatever sliver of consciousness he shared with the daemon. "It's going to take some getting used to. But then again, so would being dead."

Shane offered him a hand to help him to his feet. "This is better than dead."

"Yeah," Lucas replied, dusting himself off. "Definitely better." He glanced around the room, from the smoking shell of the downed robot to its newly fostered creations. "We're done here. Let's get gone."

EPILOGUE

"You think we did the right thing?" Lucas asked as he and Shane took a week off from their travels, opting to stay at Fort Getty to recover. It wasn't a vacation; the fort needed every resident to pitch in on the everyday chores, but the break from the road was something both men sorely needed.

"You're here. The bots have a new keeper. We've made worse decisions," Shane replied and took a slug of the raw homemade whiskey that was Major Harris's pride and joy.

Lucas's hand went to his chest. Beneath his shirt, the twisted pink scars of a fatal burn stretched across his skin like lightning. The fort's doctor had remarked he'd never seen a man struck like that who lived, but all the diagnostics he could run showed Lucas to be in perfect health.

Perhaps a little too perfect.

"Doc said my vitals are better than what he'd expect from a teenager," Lucas said. "As if I'd stopped aging. Or actually got younger."

"All those stories about the miracle water at Lourdes? The

Fountain of Youth? If those were daemons, then yeah, you might be bulletproof and immortal. Damn."

"I'm not going to test either theory, but…it's weird to think about."

"I'm glad you're still here." Shane took another swig.

"So am I. Surprised, but glad."

"I think that the daemon—"

"Rocky."

"What?"

"Rocky. That's what I call the daemon. Because it came from High Rock."

"Rocky?"

"You have a better idea?" Lucas challenged.

"He's your daemon, you get to name him," Shane conceded, secretly thrilled to be back to their old familiar banter. "Anyhow, I think…Rocky…is saprophytic."

"That sounds dirty."

Shane rolled his eyes. "Like Spanish moss. It coexists with its tree hosts in a mutually beneficial relationship. Unlike a parasite, which kills its host."

"You figured this out, how?"

"Doc and I did a little digging through his reference books, while you were resting," Shane admitted.

"Am I different?" Lucas asked, looking away as he took a sip of his own drink. "I mean, I can tell that Rocky's in here with me, way in the back. Sometimes, when I dream, I know the memories aren't mine. I know we had to let Doc in on it, but other people? I don't think they'll take it well. Can you tell that I'm not…human…anymore?"

Lucas didn't look at Shane, but Lucas was certain Shane could hear the worry in his voice.

"You're you," Shane replied with a shrug. "Same old asshole I've known all my life. Except—"

"What?" Lucas asked, clearly nervous.

"You sing now."

"I *sing?*"

"Well, Rocky does. The daemon's song that I heard coming from High Rock? Now it comes from you."

"So other daemons will know?"

"Almost certainly."

"Is that a good thing, or a bad thing?" Lucas asked.

"Probably good, on the whole. It might keep the bad daemons from fucking with us. If there are creatures out there that also pick up on the song, they might think twice about causing trouble. We still really don't know what you could do in a fight, with the daemon's energy inside you."

"Well, shit. I'm going to have to think about that for a while because Rocky says he's never possessed anyone before."

They sat in companionable silence for a few minutes, looking up at a night sky that seemed much darker and star-filled without city lights. "When we go out again, where do you want to go?" Shane asked.

"Figured we'd go to Fort Detrick and see about those zombies," Lucas replied, sipping his whiskey again. "Maybe some weres, too, if Harris's intel is right."

"Fine by me. Sounds like our kind of party," Shane answered with a grin, letting Lucas know that daemon or not, everything was business as usual.

ABOUT THE AUTHORS

Gail Z. Martin writes epic fantasy, urban fantasy, steampunk, and comedic horror for Solaris Books, Orbit Books, Falstaff Books, Worldbuilders Press, SOL Publishing and Darkwind Press. Her series include Darkhurst, Assassins of Landria, Chronicles of the Necromancer, Ascendant Kingdoms Saga, Deadly Curiosities and the Night Vigil. As Morgan Brice, she writes urban fantasy MM paranormal romance, including the Witchbane,Badlands, and Treasure Trail series.

Larry N. Martin writes and co-authors science fiction, steampunk, and urban fantasy for Solaris Books, Falstaff Books, Worldbuilders Press, and SOL Publishing. His newest book is *The Shattered Crown,* a portal gaming fantasy. He also is the author of *Salvage Rat,* the first in a new space opera series.

Together Gail and Larry co-author the steampunk series *Iron and Blood: The Jake Desmet Adventures,* a series of related short stories: *The Storm & Fury Adventures,* and the snarky monster hunter series *Spells, Salt, and Steel* set in the New Templar Knights universe. Short stories also appear in the anthologies *Cinched: Imagination Unbound, Weird Wild West,*

Alien Artifacts, Afterpunk, and many others. Also watch for another new series coming soon: The Joe Mack Shadow Council Files.

You can learn more about Gail and Larry at GailZMartin.com LarryNMartin.com, or join their newsletter and get free excerpts at http://eepurl.com/dd5XLj.

STAY IN TOUCH

Keep up with all the newest releases and appearance news from Larry & Gail by visiting GailZMartin.com and signing up for their newsletter!

FALSTAFF BOOKS

Printed in Great Britain
by Amazon

39773365R00078